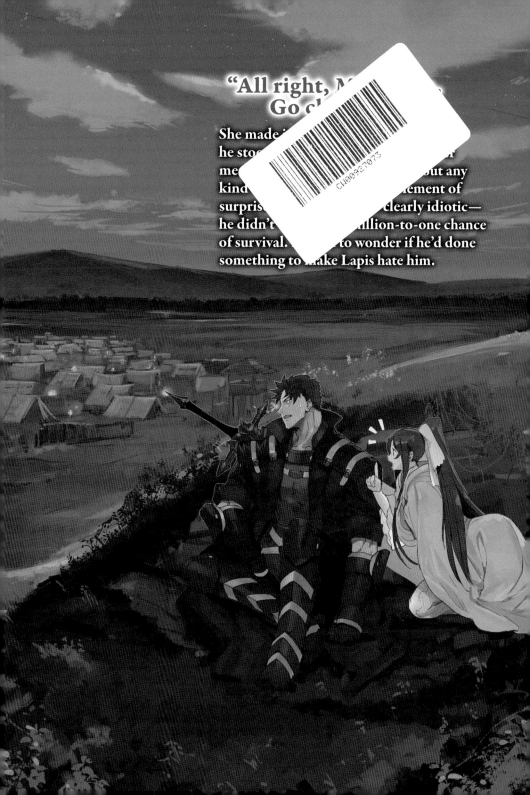

"All right, M̶_̶_̶_̶_̶_̶.
Go c̶_̶_̶_̶_̶."

She made i̶_̶_̶_̶_̶_̶_̶_̶_̶_̶_̶_̶_̶_̶
he stoc̶_̶_̶_̶_̶_̶_̶_̶_̶_̶_̶_̶_̶_̶
me̶_̶_̶_̶_̶_̶_̶_̶_̶_̶_̶_̶_̶ out any
kind̶_̶_̶_̶_̶_̶_̶_̶_̶_̶_̶ement of
surpris̶_̶_̶_̶_̶_̶_̶_̶ clearly idiotic—
he didn't̶_̶_̶_̶_̶_̶illion-to-one chance
of survival.̶_̶_̶_̶ to wonder if he'd done
something to make Lapis hate him.

Lapis

A priest who served as the healer of the first party Loren ever worked with. Owing to a certain secret of hers, she decided to stick around with Loren after that.

Scena

A young girl whom Loren and Lapis saved in the forest, though after that, a ritual turned her into a Lifeless King, and she went on a wild rampage. She was defeated by Loren, but she evaded destruction by possessing him.

Loren

A former mercenary who became an adventurer after his mercenary company fell to ruin. He boasts enough physical strength to easily swing around a sword as tall as he is. While he generally looks rough around the edges, he has a surprisingly wide breadth of knowledge. Scena, a Lifeless King, has taken up residence in his soul.

Feuille

An elf boy who Loren and Lapis rescued from a bandit camp. They are escorting him back to an elven settlement in the Black Forest.

"Might I ask your name?"

Loren couldn't bring himself to speak.

"I'm Gula Gluttonia. They used to call me the dark god of gluttony or somethin', and some adventurer sealed me away because of it. Now here I am, revived. That a good enough answer for you?"

THE Strange Adventure OF A Broke MERCENARY

THE Strange Adventure OF A Broke MERCENARY

NOVEL 4

WRITTEN BY

Mine

ILLUSTRATED BY

peroshi

Airship

Seven Seas Entertainment

KUITSUME YOHEI NO GENSO KITAN Volume 4
©Mine
Illustrations by peroshi
Originally published in Japan by HOBBY JAPAN, Tokyo.
English translation rights arranged with HOBBY JAPAN, Tokyo,
through TOHAN CORPORATION, Tokyo.

Seven Seas press and purchase enquiries can be sent to
Marketing Manager Lianne Sentar at press@gomanga.com.
Information regarding the distribution and purchase of
digital editions is available from Digital Manager CK Russell
at digital@gomanga.com.

Follow Seven Seas Entertainment online at
sevenseasentertainment.com.

TRANSLATION: Roy Nukia
ADAPTATION: N. Candon
COVER DESIGN: Hanase Qi
INTERIOR LAYOUT & DESIGN: Clay Gardner
COPY EDITOR: Linda Lombardi
PROOFREADER: Meg van Huygen
LIGHT NOVEL EDITOR: E.M. Candon
PREPRESS TECHNICIAN: Melanie Ujimori
PRINT MANAGER: Rhiannon Rasmussen-Silverstein
PRODUCTION MANAGER: Lissa Pattillo
EDITOR-IN-CHIEF: Julie Davis
ASSOCIATE PUBLISHER: Adam Arnold
PUBLISHER: Jason DeAngelis

ISBN: 978-1-63858-155-0
Printed in Canada
First Printing: March 2022
10 9 8 7 6 5 4 3 2 1

THE STRANGE ADVENTURE OF A BROKE MERCENARY

Fantasie Geshichte von
Söldner in großer Armut

CONTENTS

PROLOGUE
Listening to Tales of the Unruined

THE RUMOR that a certain school had gone under was not, in fact, spreading.

Not too long ago, that school had suffered considerable damage to both its student body and its property, but it seemed even that wasn't enough to shake its foundations.

Or maybe that muscles-for-brains headmaster's just surprisingly competent, Loren thought as he allowed the red-haired Claes to treat him to drinks at a bar in Kaffa.

Loren had been running into Claes quite often since he started this adventurer business. Now that Claes had been personally saved by Loren's efforts, it seemed he felt rather grateful. Probably out of some sense of debt, he'd proposed picking up Loren's tab of his own volition.

At first, Loren hadn't been so enthusiastic about it. After receiving the same proposal numerous times, though, he realized Claes would only be satisfied if Loren tagged along at least once.

"But I don't know what to think about drinking in the middle of the day," he muttered to himself.

Of course, Loren did a little day drinking now and again, but it was a different story when someone else was putting him up to it. The liquor swishing around his mug was quite a bit more expensive than his usual swill, so much so that he felt a little apologetic about drinking it for free.

Across the table, Claes picked at the sausage platter he'd ordered as a snack, drinking the same exact expensive liquor. He seemed quite surprised when he caught Loren's murmur of doubt.

"What's with that face?" Loren asked.

"Nothing. I just didn't think you were the sort of person who got hung up about that."

Do I really look that loose? Loren tilted his head. At the very least, he couldn't remember many mercenaries who drank before work. Parading drunk onto the battlefield was a quick way to get dead, so most learned to show a bit of moderation.

That being said, there were always exceptions, drunkards who indulged regardless of whether it was before, during, or after a job. Loren was, however, best off not using those folks as reference.

Loren spoke a little of his mercenary days to say as much.

"Adventurers have plenty of time to kill between quests. I guess that's different from mercenaries," Claes said with a smile.

That smile on his pretty face made Loren think, *I see, if I were a lady, I might have fallen for him just like that*. However, he was a man; while he was a little impressed, those feelings stopped at a disinterested snort.

Claes continued, "It's not a bad deal to let loose now and then, sipping on expensive liquor while the sun is high."

Loren's eyes dropped to the purple liquid filling his cup to the brim. The cheap ale he usually drank was mainly made from fermented grain, but this brew was processed from grapes. The swill offered at most pubs was simply stuffed into barrels, then went straight from the barrel to the mug. In contrast, this liquor was carefully packaged bottle by bottle. Maybe that was what made it even more expensive than its base fruits.

"Waargenberg wine," Claes said. "Word on the street is that this year's batch is exceptional."

"Waargenberg? Where's that?" Loren asked, which made Claes freeze for a moment.

Claes sat there, unmoving, looking at Loren as if he couldn't believe what he had just heard. Loren glared back, not quite in the mood to be stared at and finding something a tad irritating about Claes's eyes.

Panicked at the thought of upsetting Loren, Claes waved his hands and said, "No, um, err. You know where we are, right?"

"Kaffa?"

"And Kaffa belongs to the Kingdom of Waargenberg, located in the southwest of the continent. Does that ring any bells?"

Oh really, was all Loren thought about that. Even he realized he was being a bit too apathetic, but after living so long without roots, how else could he be? The name of the country he was in or the battlefield he was headed to only mattered to the company captain and the higher-ups. To a mercenary who lived without ties to any nation, it was far more important to think about defeating the enemy before his eyes rather than memorizing the name of this or that place name. That attitude hadn't changed much when Loren became an adventurer.

"If your fame as an adventurer rises, you can get called on for quests from the government or the nobles," said Claes. "I think you should look into these things a bit."

"When I don't even have the money to feed myself, you honestly think that day's gonna come?" Loren wasn't going to say it was impossible. However, even if that day ever did arrive, it was far, far away.

"I don't think it's too far off! Not with your sword skills."

"My brute strength's all I've got going for me. I'm sure anyone could do the same as long as they could swing this thing." Loren tapped the black sword beside him.

Claes replied with an ambiguous smile and a powerless laugh. Loren's main weapon was just as ridiculously heavy as it looked, and Claes had to wonder if anyone in the world apart from Loren could do much more than lift it, if that.

At the very least, if anyone ever asked Claes if he could swing it around as freely as Loren could, Claes would immediately answer "never." He knew that just from looking at the thing.

"I learned normal swordplay, once upon a time... Just wasn't for me," Loren confessed.

"I'd like to see that."

"It ain't a show. Our captain just said, 'This is just hopeless,' and gave up on me."

A peculiar sensation came over Loren the moment he mentioned the captain. He'd fought under that very captain not so long ago. Back then, he couldn't ever have imagined that the company would fall to ruin, that he would be separated from his comrades, and that he would be working as an adventurer in who knew where. That was all an undeniable reality to him now: he didn't know if anyone from the company was still alive, and he had escaped alone to what was apparently Kaffa-in-the-Kingdom-of-Waargenberg, where he was barely making a living.

To top it all off, he had a demon following him around. Fate was a fickle mistress.

"Any word about your comrades from that company of yours?" Claes asked.

"I don't know, and I don't feel like looking into it. Unlike farmers and townsfolk, mercenaries like me have no way of identifying themselves. Couldn't find them even if I tried."

Maybe the term "carefree wanderer" had a nice ring to it, but a mercenary's status and identity were never guaranteed. Their company was the only authority that would vouch for them, and if the company dissolved, that safety net disappeared.

"Well," Loren continued, "with all the strange folk I've been coming across lately, I might just run into them one of these days."

"I hope so."

"Even if that happens, I don't plan to go back to being a mercenary. Don't feel up to using human lives as a meal ticket anymore, and I've got a promise to keep."

"All right, enough gloomy stories!" A girl with long black hair abruptly intruded on the conversation, claiming the seat beside Loren. "Who exactly benefits from two men getting depressed in the corner of a bar at noon?"

She was dressed in priestly vestments and her orderly features had assembled themselves into an exasperated expression. She sat down, motioned a passing waitress toward Loren's cup, and handed over a silver coin to order the same.

"Find any good quests, Lapis?" Loren asked.

The girl, or rather Lapis, shrugged. She had readily tagged along when she heard Loren would be drinking on Claes's tab. While the two men drank, she busied herself at the bar's counter, hunting for their next quest. Given her reaction, the results were not to her satisfaction.

"I'm not feeling any of them," she said. "But that's just how it is, sometimes."

When the waitress returned, Lapis took the cup from her tray, thanked her, and downed half of it in one gulp. Sure, the Waargenberg wine was smooth and went down easy, and neither was it particularly strong, but Loren had to wonder if Lapis would knock herself out drinking like that. Not that Lapis was a normal girl—as a demon, she innately possessed superior abilities. Maybe she'd be just fine. He decided to hold his tongue.

"I wouldn't mind treating you too," Claes said, seeing that Lapis had paid for herself.

Lapis wiped her mouth with the back of her hand, put her cup on the table, and scoffed. "I wouldn't mind Loren treating me, but if it's you, I must decline."

"You know I can't..." Loren muttered.

His last quest hadn't put him in the red, shockingly. Just barely, though, and he'd hardly made a profit. Loren's wallet was as desolate as ever.

"It's the principle of things. I don't want to be treated by someone leading around a harem—a man who wishes to surround himself with mistresses even after taking a wife."

"Looks like she hates you," Loren told Claes.

"I have a seething distaste for snakes, but compared to Claes, I would prefer them."

Lapis's evaluation of Claes was low. Understandably so. Loren let her berate the man without a word in his defense. Claes had mellowed out a bit compared to when they first met, but his womanizing and slovenliness persisted. Perhaps he didn't intend to take himself in hand on those matters at all.

That was a problem for Claes and those around him, not anything an outsider could weigh in on. Loren decided he wouldn't think anything of it, if it didn't bring him any harm. Of course, it was clear to see why any woman would recognize Claes as a natural enemy, so he didn't plan on stopping Lapis either.

"I'm just here to accompany Mr. Loren," Lapis concluded. "You can ignore me."

"Oh... Well, all right."

"Oh, but I do have a high opinion of your *Boost*, if nothing else," Lapis assured him. "I will gladly use it again should anything happen."

Claes laughed nervously.

During a past job, while they were fleeing from an enemy, she had tossed Claes onto a horse and made him use his *Boost* ability to draw out its equine potential. Armed with a whip, Lapis had ensured he kept at it for an entire night.

Taking her eyes off Claes—who was still laughing stiffly—Lapis turned to Loren.

"There weren't any promising requests, but unless we work, Mr. Loren, you'll have no means of supporting yourself."

"I don't want to get any further in the hole either."

This was the promise between Loren and Lapis: they would work together until Loren had paid his debt to her. Her terms were generous, and she wasn't urgently demanding any money, but the sum had reached over thirty gold coins. Loren didn't want to heap anything else on that pile.

"I don't really mind, but it might get awkward between us if I keep lending you money, so I do see the value in labor."

"But there weren't any good quests, right?" Loren asked.

Nothing good awaited them if they took the wrong request. Every quest Loren took—or rather, every quest Lapis brought him—seemed far more difficult than anything suited for copper-rank adventurers like him. He couldn't begin to imagine how bad these quests must be if even Lapis was avoiding them.

"There weren't any quests, but something nice just occurred to me," Lapis said, her face simply sparkling. The more she glowed, the longer the shadows stretched across Loren's face.

He had a vague inkling that this would once again lead to something outrageous. Unfortunately, he had another inkling that he wouldn't be able to avoid the trouble. Loren gave up and downed his cup of wine, resolving to hear out her idea.

1 Paying Heed to a Choice

"I'VE GIVEN A BIT OF THOUGHT to why you keep failing quests. You should be more than skilled enough, Mr. Loren, yet somehow the results don't show it."

They were in the same party, so surely Lapis was equally to blame—not that Loren would say that out loud. There was no way she didn't already understand that. She was deliberately dancing around the subject.

Is she teasing, or is she trying to start something? Regardless, Loren continued staring at her without showing any reaction, and her hopeful expression gradually dimmed. Eventually, the glimmer in her eyes turned to disappointment.

"Umm, I don't think you should blame a party's failure on a single member..." said Claes, looking between the two, who seemed locked in a stalemate.

Lapis glared at him like a watchdog confronting an intruder. "I know that. I was fishing for a reaction, good grief." She seemed a little angry, but not nearly as much as she was pretending to be.

When Loren nudged her to continue, she immediately shifted gears back to this brilliant idea of hers. "In short, you fail because you take quests."

"What's that supposed to mean?"

"You can't fail if you don't take any," she proudly proclaimed.

"Are you drunk already?" Loren retorted coldly.

There was a clean sort of logic to it. The very act of accepting quests created the risk of failing them. In fact, it made perfect sense—excluding the fact that avoiding quests meant avoiding work. An adventurer lived solely on the earnings from their quests; following Lapis's suggestion would mean cutting off Loren's only stream of revenue.

Not that Loren's quests were providing a satisfactory return. It was hard to say he was even making a living. When he admitted that to himself, a dark and heavy air fell over him.

"Umm, what part of that was a good idea? It sounds to me like you want him to quit being an adventurer," Claes spoke in Loren's stead, as it seemed Loren had lost the will to object.

Lapis must have realized she'd stepped on a landmine; she didn't lash out at Claes as she answered. "Put simply, we'll just have to take on a job that isn't a quest."

What is she talking about? Loren wondered, but Claes clapped his hands together in triumphant understanding. In fact, it seemed like Loren was the only one who couldn't see where the conversation was headed. He didn't care if it was the priest or the swordsman, he just hoped someone would explain.

Claes obliged. "I believe Ms. Lapis is suggesting going out

into the fields and hunting monsters for their bounties. Is that right?"

"Yes, the skirt-chaser has it right." Lapis's insult was as casual as her nod.

Loren still looked doubtful, so she elaborated. Strictly speaking, bounty hunting wasn't questing. No one in particular requested a party for the job, but the adventurers' guild had a permanent arrangement. The guild would pay a set sum to adventurers who slew monsters and brought in the right bits and pieces of beastly corpses to prove it.

Notably, this sum was paid as a bonus on top of the normal rewards for monsters hunted in the midst of a quest. There were some adventurers like Loren who misunderstood, believing the quests and the bounties went hand in hand. But the fact of the matter was that the guild would exchange monster parts for money regardless of when or why they were offered up.

Hunting monsters benefited the public order. By insisting they play a part in the effort, the adventurers' guild improved their public image. Most countries with guild chapters subsidized monster hunting to a degree, and most monster materials ultimately ended up with the guild. Loren and Lapis could expect to profit quite a bit through the sale of fiendish claws or fangs.

Overall, countries received protection at a low fee, civilians enjoyed a lower risk of monster attacks, adventurers still got paid when there were no quests, and the adventurers' guild could boost both its funds and reputation. The system benefited all parties concerned.

"I suggest hunting monsters along the highway north of Kaffa," Lapis concluded.

Monster encounter rates would be low on the actual highway. Instead, she suggested plotting a course parallel to it, a short distance off the path.

Still, thought Loren, *if we follow the highway north, there's a chance we won't run into anything at all.* If that happened, he would have no monster parts to exchange. No income. On top of that, it would take several days to cover the distance, and he would need to buy the necessary supplies.

There was no way Loren could ignore these expenses and risks—he simply didn't have the money to spare. He looked at Lapis, quizzical, but she had an answer prepared.

"Even if we don't run into anything, our end destination will be the Black Forest. There should be plenty of monsters there, so I doubt we'll return completely empty-handed. Even if we somehow do come back with nothing to show for it, we'll map out our route and report it to the guild. They'll cover some of our costs for that alone."

If they didn't meet any monsters at all, that would mean they had stumbled upon a safe route through those dangerous lands. Information on this passage would prove quite valuable in itself, according to Lapis. Who exactly it would prove valuable to, she wouldn't say. Loren had to wonder if the map would be sold to the sort of people who couldn't exactly use the main roads.

"Whatever happens, you should be able to make some money," Lapis said.

"As long as we don't lose our bag of monster parts again."

Seeing that Loren was intent on taking the conversation in a negative direction, Lapis and Claes both offered wry smiles. It was often said one should plan with the worst-case scenario in mind, but Loren was starting to feel his pessimism was almost pathological.

"It shouldn't be too dangerous near the highway, so I think we'll be fine," offered Lapis.

"Even if it's not an official job, the Adventurer's Guild will still respect you for your contributions. I don't think it's a bad deal," Claes said.

"Let me say this beforehand—I'm not asking for *your* cooperation. Mr. Loren and I will be fine on our own." Lapis puffed herself up to better intimidate her target, not wanting to deal with Claes and his party of women for another second.

Claes easily conceded. "Yeah, I get that. I'm not gonna put a damper on your travels." He went on, "I don't know about you, but we've got money to spare. Go and enjoy your lovey-dovey trip to the Black Forest, why don't you?"

Lapis's cheeks reddened ever so slightly.

Pretending he didn't see this, Loren asked, "What sort of place is the Black Forest?"

It took a moment of Claes looking up at the ceiling, sorting through his knowledge, before he replied. "It's a decently sized forest two days' walk north of Kaffa. The trees are so thick that it's pitch-black all around if you head too far in—that's why it's called the Black Forest. The guild's confirmed a large number of monsters living there, and there are rumors of elves and fairies as well."

"Hmm. Elves, eh?" Loren asked.

That immediately brought to mind Nym, a member of a silver-rank adventurer party they'd once worked with. She was lanky and used a bow; she couldn't possibly have been any more elvish. It was generally known that elves boasted beautiful faces, with ears long and pointed like dagger blades. They were also lightly built and constructed their settlements in the forests far from human habitation, where they had their own unique culture.

Honestly, the elvish community was rather insular, and it was quite rare to find an elf who chose to live in human society like Nym did.

"If you're thinking of poking around for elves, I'd quit while you're ahead," Claes said. "They're not citizens of the kingdom, so the kingdom's laws don't apply. They control the forests with their own set of rules. You'll have hell to pay if they catch you trespassing. Sure, they're beautiful, but it just ain't worth it."

Loren frowned. "I'm not you."

Claes fell into yet another slump, cut to the bone by Loren's words. Loren didn't need anyone to lecture him about common sense—only the foolish and the shameless would go after an elf in the forest. Loren didn't consider himself either.

"Just ignore the indiscriminate philanderer. How about it, Mr. Loren? I don't think it's a bad proposal," Lapis said.

"Let's see..."

Loren considered it. After a string of failures, it was only human nature to detest the thing he kept failing at. A change of pace was necessary, now and again. Put like that, taking it easy for a few days didn't sound so bad, even if he couldn't turn a profit.

On the other hand, that last quest—while terrible—had been something like successful. Loren didn't think things were so dire that he needed to take a break. On the third, demonic hand, though, he didn't want to compromise Lapis's goodwill. That decided it. He pretended not to have any second thoughts at all.

"All right, got it," he said. "Let's give it a shot."

"That settles it! Then I'll need to buy food supplies, among other things."

Lapis would leave the riddle of packing to Lapis. Some might say he was slacking off, but he didn't have the money to scrape together supplies anyway. He was dependent on her wallet no matter what.

"Sorry about that," he told her. "I'll let you choose what we're taking."

"You'll at least carry the bags, won't you?" Lapis asked, and Loren immediately nodded.

If he couldn't provide in money, he could at least offer his labor. Otherwise, he'd be totally reliant on her.

"Then let's get shopping. It's best to act while the motivation is still fresh."

"I don't want to walk when I've got alcohol in me, but...whatever." Loren's head was a bit foggy, but he stood and turned to Claes, who was still sulking. "Well, you heard the lady. We'll be off now."

"Yeah, take care." Claes lifted his head just enough to see them off.

Lapis dragged Loren away into town, the picture of a settled, well-adjusted couple. Wrestling with just a little envy, Claes pressed his cup to his lips. *Maybe one of my party members can console me*, he thought absentmindedly, unaware that the cold in Lapis's eyes would have dropped to absolute zero if she heard that.

After a day spent gathering the necessary supplies, Loren and Lapis set off from Kaffa the next morning. They were staring down several days on the road ahead, which meant quite a bit of food for quite a bit of silver. Ultimately, Lapis had to rent a donkey to carry it all.

On outings like this, it was common for adventurers to either rent a pack animal or hire a porter—a specialist at transporting goods. There were, of course, the rare exceptions, which usually came when a party had members to spare. Those lucky few distributed supplies amongst themselves, lessening the load on any one person. Lapis didn't feel like taking on any new members to play pack mule, nor did she want to pay anyone to do so.

"It's just the two of us, for once. I don't feel like adding anyone else to the mix," she said.

Loren couldn't say if this was the right decision. But if this was what Lapis wanted, he respected her opinion. He took the donkey's reins without argument.

With a bag on Loren's back and the donkey hauling everything else, they were ready to set off. They left through Kaffa's main gate and headed down the north road at a leisurely pace.

"We can release the donkey in case of emergency," Lapis told him. "It's apparently been trained to return to Kaffa on its own."

If they were ambushed, protecting the donkey wouldn't be high on their list of priorities. Loren was only worried that donkey vendors might take a "you break it, you buy it" approach to livestock.

"They don't make you guarantee the return," Lapis said, picking up on his concerns. "Either way, a dead donkey is far better than you holding the line and becoming a dead Loren."

"So, you didn't borrow a horse because it'll be cheaper if the donkey croaks?"

"Well, horses do go for a pretty penny."

The warhorses used by soldiers were incredibly rare, but even normal horses were expensive. A sturdy pony wasn't out of the realm of possibility, but Lapis had balked at the price tag.

"Considering speed and stamina, a horse would've been a bit better," she conceded.

"The guild must have deep pockets."

On a past quest, the adventurers' guild had casually arranged for horse-drawn wagons to carry everyone on the mission. Loren hadn't thought anything of it at the time. Now that they were haggling for themselves, though, he was reminded of the power the organization boasted.

"I heard it was two days each way," he said. "Are we camping out along the way?"

There were tents and sleeping bags on the donkey's back. Loren didn't know what to think about a man and a woman camping out alone together. In his short stint as an adventurer, he had sort of picked up that adventurers didn't put much stock in that sort of concern.

Claes wasn't the first he'd seen to nonchalantly form a party with one man and many women, sleeping all piled up in the same tent. By now, Loren knew various takes on the matter: there weren't enough tents for everyone; an adventurer could turn the tables on whoever tried to assault them; some people looked forward to their tent-fellows getting handsy. Loren wondered which view Lapis agreed with.

"Oh? You wanted to camp out with me, Mr. Loren? In that case, maybe I should have packed just the one tent. Or just the one sleeping bag?"

Tearing his eyes from Lapis's complacent smile, Loren glanced at the back of the donkey. Lapis liked her space and her own tent. As long as nothing went wrong, they wouldn't have to worry about...situations.

"I don't want to die yet," Loren said, earnest as anything, as he returned his gaze to the girl walking beside him.

Lapis puffed up her cheeks, discontented, and prodded an elbow into his side. "What does camping together have to do with a matter of life and death?"

"No, I mean, if I tried anything indecent, you'd definitely twist my head right off."

Lapis's slender arms didn't look particularly toned, but Loren knew they contained strength unimaginable. After all, Lapis was a demon whose limbs and eyes had been snatched away to seal that very power. Loren was always impressed by how functional her demon-made prosthetics turned out to be—he had seen her snap goblin necks barehanded.

It was possible that Lapis was so strong precisely because she was using artificial limbs, but she was also fixated on recovering her various parts. It was hard to imagine that her real body didn't outclass her current equipment.

And, during their last quest, Lapis had regained her left arm. Loren was understandably wary of it.

"That depends on who's doing indecent things. Please, don't make it sound like I would just twist *anyone's* head off."

"Then you're fine with me?" Loren asked.

"Wow, that was...pretty straightforward. Even I would, umm... rather have a conversation and some preparations, so..." Lapis's face reddened as she fidgeted and rubbed her fingers together.

Lapis often teased and joked around; Loren was surprised by this new reaction when he poked her right back. Feeling a bit like he'd cracked some very difficult code, he gave her a light nudge on the back. She carried on mumbling under her breath.

It took a bit before Lapis's mind clawed its way free from the labyrinthian maze of her imagination and whatnot. "There are rest towns along the way," she said at last. "We should be fine staying in the inns."

The northern road was regularly maintained, with rest towns dotted along it, only as far from each other as an average person

could walk in a day. Naturally, there was also a stop near the Black Forest, about two days away. Lapis intended to use it as a base of operations for their hunts.

"I'll put up with tents when it's unavoidable," Lapis continued, "but I'd rather not camp if we don't have to. I do like to sleep in a proper bed."

Loren shrugged. "I don't care either way. It wasn't too rare for us mercenaries to sleep in a huddle on the bare soil."

"That sounds like you'd be covered in sweat and grime by morning..." Lapis said, sounding rather put off. She was, in fact, correct. Loren had experienced that sweat and grime a good deal over the years, so he could only shrug at her again.

On the battlefield, Loren had been grateful to get any sleep at all. Oftentimes, even getting to sit down or shut his eyes had been an unthinkable luxury. Not that there was any point in telling Lapis this.

Even when he was covered in sweat and grime, a mercenary rarely got a chance to wash it off. Dirt was the least of his worries when he could find himself covered in blood splatter and trodden mud. Even then, he would sleep standing up and filthy if he got the chance.

"The humans are a strange set of creatures. They call themselves civilized, yet they're perfectly fine flopping into bed without showering, and they don't even build baths in their houses. What part of that is civilized?"

"Baths?" Loren repeated. "In houses?"

He knew the word bath, of course, and he knew what it meant: baths were, hypothetically, places where a large sort of tub was filled with a staggering amount of water, and then people sat around in it. Loren had never experienced this himself.

It was difficult enough to draw so much water. And he'd heard it was all heated. Just how much time, money, and magic would that take? All that just to get rid of a bit of dirt—it sounded terribly inefficient.

If cleaning was all a bath offered, a great big bucket took up far more space than it was worth. There was no way any standard household would be so wasteful. As far as Loren knew, they were only built in the palaces and estates of the upper crust.

He'd heard about regions where hot water welled up from the earth itself, where locals made a business out of natural baths, but Loren had never been to such a far-flung place.

"They generally have baths in demon houses, you know," Lapis told him. "They're so lovely, and I can't imagine why they never caught on with the humans. It's a mystery!"

"If you want to clean yourself off, a wet cloth is good enough."

That was normal. Sure, winters made the water so unbearably cold that it had to be heated. Even then, a single pail of water was more than sufficient. There was no need to have enough water to drown in.

"Baths aren't meant to be functional," Lapis insisted. "They're more like an emotional journey. You'll understand if you try it."

"Is that how it works?" Loren asked, just humoring her now. He doubted the day would ever come for him to take a bath.

"I'll make sure our next quest takes us somewhere with baths. You *must* learn how wonderful they can be."

"You're not really convincing me," he confessed.

The conversation kept up as they meandered down a path parallel to the highway. They didn't run into any of the monsters they were looking for. So far, the travel plan just ate up time on their way to the forest. Some other adventurers must have had similar ideas. Maybe parties like theirs set out at regular intervals, maintaining the safety of the whole region. Inconvenient.

"It's not all bad," Lapis said. "Now the travelers can use the roads with some peace of mind."

"Yeah, but without anything to hunt, it feels like my wallet's even lighter than usual."

"We might not turn a huge profit, but we won't suffer a loss," Lapis insisted. "Don't worry."

Unfortunately, the situation looked even more dubious around sunset. The sky tinted red, and the curtain of darkness was soon to fall. Given the encroaching twilight and the distance they'd covered, Lapis said they were sure to reach the next town soon. They were peeling their eyes for it when they saw—something.

Lapis paused. "Is that it? How should I put it...? I'm getting a strange feeling about this."

She hardly had to spell it out. At the end of the highway, where there were no hills or trees to block their view, there was one spot that remained red as the darkness fell, as if the remnants of sunset had taken up permanent residence. Black pillars stretched up toward the sky, birthed from that bright point directly on the road.

It was pretty easy for Loren to figure out what was happening at their destination. "Well, I'd say that's on fire."

"Oh good, it wasn't just me, then."

The sky turned from blue to red, from red to black, and still the ember glow remained on the horizon. This absolutely reeked of trouble.

"You might not be getting that bed of yours today," Loren said.

"I suppose that's life."

Lapis looked so heartbroken that Loren had to wonder if she was actually that torn up about it.

Standing and watching accomplished nothing. Regardless of what was happening ahead, they couldn't turn back. Before either could lose their nerve, they set off toward the blazing red light.

All that awaited them was fire and ash. What had presumably been a proper rest town not too long ago was collapsing as the fire engulfed it. Flames bloomed, and the buildings let out thunderous rumbles.

The heat of the fire wafted the thick black smoke into the sky. The entire place smelled of burning—and worse. A nauseating stench clung to the once-human silhouettes that decorated the burning houses.

"Now this is quite..."

Lapis looked shocked as she inspected the corpse at her feet. Had it been a resident of the town? It belonged to a middle-aged man, his expression of terror illuminated by the flames that had killed him.

Stooping down next to the body, Loren considered the single gash on the back of the man's shoulder and grimaced. "Hit in the back. Do you think it was a monster?"

But if it was a beast-like monster, its claws and fangs wouldn't have left this one single mark. That meant a monster with a weapon, perhaps a goblin or an orc.

Lapis took a look at the body's condition and shook her head. "The wound is too deep for a goblin and too shallow for an orc. And neither of them would have left a perfectly good body behind."

Both goblins and orcs were omnivorous, and they happily ate humans. Perhaps they would ignore the burnt-up bodies, but it was hard to believe they would leave a fresh kill without having a nibble.

"Which means this is a human's doing."

"Presumably. And quite a number they've done here." Lapis sighed, her eyes locked on one of the houses, its walls crumbling and its roof ablaze.

The presumed humans who had attacked the rest town— which wasn't particularly large—had ransacked the lot, snatching or smashing whatever they could. Once that was done, they set the town ablaze.

"Do you think there're any survivors?" Loren asked.

"If there are, they must be blessed by fortune. In fact, I'd like some of their luck for myself." Lapis tried to make it into a light quip, but her face was stiff.

Anyone would be stiff when staring down something like this, Loren thought, though this all left them with a problem. "We've lost our bed for the night."

"You have a lot of nerve to worry about that now, Mr. Loren."

"This isn't the first time I've seen this sort of thing."

Pillaged towns and villages were hardly a rare sight in the midst of war. Loren, or rather his company, hadn't engaged in the act as a matter of pride, but he'd seen other mercenaries, often those allied with his enemies, descend upon settlements with torches and ill intent. He'd also seen the aftermath.

Loren's heart wasn't so numb that he didn't feel pity, but it was hardened by experience. He knew that nothing would come of losing his mind or flying into a rage. "With the whole place burning like this, it's gonna be a while before it settles down."

"Why did they do it, do you think? Were they not also human?" Lapis asked levelly.

Loren scratched his head. He didn't have an answer for her. There were villages, and there were bandits—that was reason enough. But Loren knew that wasn't the sort of answer she wanted.

"Sorry," he finally managed. "I really couldn't tell you."

"I'm sorry, Mr. Loren. I wasn't trying to pressure you. As much as we demons are hated by the other races, we have a strong sense of camaraderie. Of course we fight for status and personal interest, but this seems to be something else entirely. So I was wondering *why*." Despite her assurances, Lapis seemed flustered.

Loren had imagined demons as living in a more brutal world. What a thing to be so mistaken about. Humans could easily pull off what even demons couldn't comprehend. Maybe he belonged to the crueler race.

"Well, if we're given sufficient reason, and push comes to shove, we demons *do* like to be at least this thorough about it."

"That's actually reassuring."

"Whoever lit the fire was naïve, though. At this rate, it'll go out before everything burns to the ground."

"I get it. Just shut up for a bit."

She'd ruined the moment, but Loren was relieved. If she hadn't made that bleak joke, it would have suggested that demons really were a kinder, more rational sort than humans. His values had nearly crumbled at their foundations.

"So what do we do now?" she asked.

"Right. For now, I guess we should look for survivors."

"And after that, we make sure there's nothing valuable lying around, yes? I expect no less from you, Mr. Loren. Let's get right to it."

"You... You know, you look like a pure and pretty priest when you keep your mouth shut."

Lapis's face turned so red he could see it even through the flames. She raised her hands to her cheeks and turned her back to Loren, mumbling to herself again.

There's no time for that, Loren thought as he watched her back. To get his own move on, he led the donkey far enough away that the flames wouldn't bother it and found a tree sturdy enough to keep it there.

Once the donkey was tethered, Lapis joined Loren in his search through the burning town. It wasn't long before the extent of the damage became clear.

"All jokes aside, they really were thorough," Lapis said. "They did so well, in fact, I would like to give them a pat on the back."

And it was indeed terrible enough to warrant her frank opinion.

There were no survivors. It was impossible to say if anyone had managed to escape during the attack, but there was not a single living soul in town. Man and woman, child and elder alike had all been mercilessly slaughtered.

Even the loot Lapis had joked about was gone. From currency to home furnishings, jewelry, and food, anything of any value at all had been taken. This plunder had been so thorough that Loren couldn't help but be impressed, even knowing how terrible it was.

"Whoever did this knew their business," Loren said.

"Is this like how you can tell the work of a master craftsman?"

"A master like this is better off dead." In short, only burning buildings and corpses remained. "Sure, it was out of the way, but shouldn't a rest town have sentries posted?"

"There were, apparently. They were burnt over there."

Lapis pointed toward the town center, where charred armored corpses had been piled up in the square. The town wasn't so big, but it was a key point on the highway. More than a dozen guards were stationed here, and they'd all been cleanly disposed of.

"Wouldn't they have had a master of the guard too? Sure, they weren't elites, but they were still soldiers, right? And they were all taken out by a group of thieves? Did they send fresh recruits or something?"

"I can't say for sure. They were all burned, after all."

"There's gotta be a sizable raiding party in the area. Seeing all they've done here, I'd say two to three hundred of them."

A brigade of bandits that large should have sparked a rumor or five, but Loren hadn't heard a single word about it in Kaffa.

"I hate to say it, but they could be disgraced mercenaries," said Loren. "After the battle that tore my company apart, a fair amount of mercs might've been left wandering."

There'd been mercenary companies on both ends of that battlefield. Loren's side had lost, but even opposing companies had suffered great damages. He could imagine a number of them were like him, forced to...consider alternatives.

It was common to fall from mercenary grace into banditry. But to form a group large enough to ransack an entire town? With those sorts of numbers, they could've just carried on as mercenaries without resorting to thievery in the first place.

"Maybe a few survivors turned bandit," Loren mused. "Then they absorbed others and kept at it as they grew."

"And they didn't think to return to mercenary work after staining their hands? How unfortunate."

The thing was, no matter how many members a company gathered, it became impossible for them to correct course to take up mercenary work once they crossed a certain line. Once they began to pursue criminal action, they would take in others similarly desperate or depraved, causing the problem to snowball until it became the avalanche before them.

As a (former) mercenary himself, Loren didn't like to think about it. Unfortunately, given the masterful raid and dead guards, nearly all of them taken out with a single strike, it was a distinct possibility. The combat ability on display was just too skilled to ignore.

"This ain't good. A few more towns are gonna fall before they send an army to do anything about it."

A criminal organization on this scale was well beyond what a small settlement could deal with. Eventually, someone—the kingdom?—would have to take notice and put together a policing force in earnest. But Loren could only imagine how many casualties would pile up before then.

"That sounds troublesome. Do you want to go crush them?"

Lapis put that suggestion out into the world a bit too casually, if you asked Loren. It took him a moment for him to catch up with her.

He blinked at her for a moment, unsure they were reading the same book, much less on the same page, then smiled bitterly. "Now hold on. If I'm right, we're up against at least two hundred battle-hardened mercenaries. That's not the sort of problem the two of us can tackle."

"Then you're going to sit back and watch until the military makes its move?" Lapis asked. "Not that it matters to me."

Loren struggled to give her an answer. He didn't nurse any heroic aspirations. He figured himself for a Decent Samaritan—he'd help out if he saw someone in trouble, sure—but no more than that. It wasn't in his nature to overlook suffering or rising casualties, but he wasn't optimistic enough to stick his neck out to tempt death.

At his silence, Lapis continued, "Our best bet is to return to Kaffa tomorrow, and head straight for the soldier outpost... But I do wonder how long it will take them to respond."

"I think you know the answer to that. Doesn't mean there's anything we can do about it."

"Is it really impossible? Between the two of us...do you really think we don't have anything to offer?"

<*Mister!*> chimed the girl always in the corner of Loren's eye. <*With me around, you'll be fine even if you do die! I can make an undead of you yet!*>

I'd rather not be an undead, he retorted. Then looked up at the sky and gave it some thought. Giving up didn't feel good. Today's losses weren't his to deal with, but the residents of the town were surely turning in their graves—or lack thereof. The dead never had but a single request for their last witnesses.

"Revenge... Right..."

There was no need to wipe out the whole two hundred-something lot. Loren could deal enough damage to slow them down. Hell, if he played his cards right, he could maybe force the group to splinter into smaller, more scattered threats that the town sentries could actually deal with.

It might even save some lives.

"Maybe. We'll at least need to thank them for ruining our night's sleep, or it won't sit right with me."

"If you're going to do it, then time is of the essence, Mr. Loren. The bandits will have let their guard down as they party over today's loot."

Lapis stood still in the dark, watching the burning town with a sinister smile on her face. While Loren smiled back at her, he knew for a fact she was a demon through and through.

THE Strange Adventure OF A Broke MERCENARY

2 Discovery to Looting

THE BANDIT CAMP was surprisingly easy to spot—mostly because they hadn't made any attempt to conceal it. On the other hand, by sheer numbers they were a force to be reckoned with; their combat potential rivaled that of a small army. Until the kingdom mustered a force large enough to quell their looting, nothing in the area presented a threat to the bandits. What was there to hide from?

"I was expecting this, but seeing them firsthand is something else," Lapis murmured.

They were about a stound—one-twelfth of a day—out from the destroyed town. The bandits had lit a large fire right in the middle of the open plains, so imposing a sight that their lax security was unlikely to get them in any trouble.

"They're doing whatever they please, but I doubt they're going at it without any thought at all," Lapis muttered, frustrated. With nowhere nearer to hide, they were keeping low in a slight depression just out of range of the camp's firelight.

Since two hundred bandits weren't worried about head-on confrontations, their main concern would be surprise attacks and traps. Rather than choosing terrain in which to hide, which would hinder their own view, they set up a camp that ensured full control of their surroundings. Were they really canny enough to do that on purpose? Impossible to say, but the results spoke for themselves. It would be safer for Loren and Lapis to operate on the assumption that these bandits knew their stuff.

"We can't just think of them like they're idiots. We should accept that they're a little clever when we make our move," said Lapis.

"Yeah, that's all well and good. But I can't really see our angle here."

If they came out of hiding, the lookouts would see them. Even if they wanted to cobble together a plan, there was nothing but open fields all around. No cover, no distractions, no nothing.

Loren was a mercenary of considerable skill, and he was more or less aware of that. What he wasn't conceited enough to think was he could cut through one hundred foes, let alone double that.

"The cliché would be to attack with fire or water, but I don't see how we're doing that here. Even if we could set up a trap, we can't make something big enough to take out the whole lot."

"You sound pretty knowledgeable, Mr. Loren."

"I've been on both sides of this coin before. And this bet's no good."

There was nothing nearby to burn, and no river or marsh to lure the bandits into. Empty plains stretched in every direction, granting no options for either offense or defense. That did go for both sides, and it would have been a different story if they were equally matched. Unfortunately, the gap between them was despair-inducingly wide, with nothing to fill it.

"You have a point. Of course, I could always use a bit of large-scale magic to annihilate them, even if it means overexerting myself."

"You can use magic like that?" Loren asked.

"Who do you think I am? Even if I don't have my limbs and eyes, I'm still a powerful demon. I even have my left arm back now."

Lapis waggled her left hand as she said this, but Loren found it difficult to believe. He knew that powerful magicians could turn a war on its head, but taking out two hundred enemies with one spell? That was a fairy tale.

"Of course, it wouldn't be without paying a hefty price. I'd like to avoid that if possible. And so, Mr. Loren, there's one thing I want to ask you."

They were huddled in a small indent, keeping as still and small as possible. Lapis stared hard at him, well within the boundaries of his personal space. Even in the darkness of the night, with only the faint glow of the distant camp, Loren could see it in her eyes. She was looking right through him; she knew about Scena.

"I believe we should put all our cards on the table. What do you think?" she asked.

Loren had never *told* her about Scena, the girl who had become an undead monster and now lived within him—or rather, within his astral body.

He had been saved a few times by Scena's power over death, and he was pretty sure Lapis already had it all figured out. She had merely pretended she didn't until he was willing to cough up a proper explanation.

Bringing it up now meant she was placing her bets on Scena's power—likely because there was no other alternative.

"It's reasonable for you to be wary of me," Lapis said. "I understand that I'm no one to trifle with. It's just a little sad that you don't trust me..."

"No, well, you know..."

She seemed truly let down, her face clouded over, and Loren felt guilty for ever having kept the secret.

"However, considering our current predicament, I think it's time to yield and offer me some information. How does that sound to you?"

Scena sent him one last thought. <*I think we should just be honest with her about it, Mister. It hurts my heart to keep her out of the loop.*>

It seemed she agreed with his feelings on the matter. It seemed to Loren that he wouldn't get a better opportunity to come clean.

"It's about Scena," he said. "The girl we failed to save on that quest..."

Lapis cut him off, "Understood. I take it that means you're finally ready to talk?" Taken aback, Loren nodded. Lapis went on. "Then am I right in assuming that Ms. Scena used her powers as a Lifeless King to rent a room within your astral body? That your soul usually serves as a cover so it's hard to tell, but if she exudes her astral body, she can use a portion of her powers?"

"So you already knew."

Of course she did.

"There's a big difference between having a hunch and receiving confirmation," Lapis told him, her voice low and her face serious.

"Are you able to see Scena?" Loren asked.

Lapis shook her head. "I can't. I felt you giving off a strange aura, and I thought that aura resembled that of the Lifeless King we encountered. Later, when you used those abilities, I got a somewhat clearer grasp of the situation."

"That's still amazing."

"Oh, I'm not *that* great. And so. Now we can put a plan together." Lapis smiled and placed a hand on Loren's shoulders. Then, before he could grasp her meaning, she nonchalantly told him: "All right, Mr. Loren. Go charge in."

"Hey, now... You want me to die?"

She made it sound so easy. From where he stood, rushing two hundred former mercenaries alone wouldn't turn out any kind of pretty, even with the element of surprise on his side. It was clearly idiotic—he didn't even have a million-to-one chance of survival. He had to wonder if he'd done something to make Lapis hate him.

"I'll provide support, don't worry."

"But I'm still...gonna die, right?"

"The match will be settled once you cut down the first few."

She didn't seem to be joking around, and it didn't sound like she wanted to send Loren to his death. Even still, he didn't see any chance of victory.

In contrast to his anxiety, Lapis looked completely convinced.

"I wouldn't attempt this plan if it were you alone, Mr. Loren. But it should be a different matter with Ms. Scena. I think we have a good shot."

"You're serious..."

The two of them stood no chance against two hundred. Twenty of them wouldn't have stood a chance, but here Lapis proclaimed her confidence in Loren on his own. To be honest, he didn't really get her angle, but she seemed absolutely certain. Not only that, but Loren didn't have any better ideas. Unable to refute her, his only options were to take her offer or turn and leave.

"This is crazy talk. Can I believe you?"

"Just leave it to me, Mr. Loren. I don't plan on losing you here, and I don't plan to be done in by bandits." She patted her chest, everything he could read in her expression devoid of lies or hesitation.

I'll trust her then, he decided, lowering his sword from his back and gripping the hilt with both hands.

"Mr. Loren, I cannot converse with Ms. Scena. Is she able to hear my words through you?"

"Yeah, she said she shares my sight and other senses."

"Then please listen to me, Ms. Scena. I want you to make some good allies. Would you be able to do that? If you can't, please tell me."

<Umm... Yes, understood. Tell her I can do it.>

"She gave the okay," Loren answered in Scena's stead.

Lapis nodded, her eyes turning to the bandit camp.

No change at the camp. The bandits hadn't noticed Loren or Lapis yet—at least, no alarm had been raised, and there were still sentries patrolling at regular intervals.

"Then let's begin. We'll rain hell upon those bastards who ruined our beds and our supper."

She delivered this line so deadpan that Loren nearly tumbled over where he stood.

She looked at him curiously, and he answered with a wry smile. "Real petty, all of a sudden."

"What are you talking about, Mr. Loren? Grudges driven by food are among the worst variety thereof. And now we have our night's sleep lost on top of that. After such insult, we'll see them dancing with the devils in hell one way or another."

"What about avenging the townsfolk?"

Lapis looked at Loren as if she had only just remembered the carnage. Her lips curled into a malicious grin. "Oh, if you want to add that dreadful whatnot to the pile, we shouldn't even give them the chance to repent."

"I'm starting to pity them."

"That's not a good habit, Mr. Loren. I need you to be merciless, levelheaded, and absolutely inhumane."

"Why do I gotta be inhumane?"

He shuddered to imagine what sort of inhumanity a demon could think up.

Without a twitch in her expression, Lapis said, "Please don't complain when the results are inhumane regardless."

"What exactly are you putting me up to?"

"No different from the usual. Confront the enemy, slay the enemy. That's all there is to it."

If that was really all there was to it, that certainly was their routine. Lapis even prepared a few familiar blessings and spells to support him.

"I'll leave the timing to you," she told him. "I'll provide support when I can."

"Fine, we'll go with that. I'll be prepared for the worst."

A large body and a massive sword—yet he moved unimaginably quickly with both as he slipped from the cavity into the night air. He didn't get far before the keen-eyed lookouts spotted him. Archers gathered to deal with this suspicious intruder.

I'll be filled with arrows at this rate, Loren thought. Lucky for him, the moment before they unleashed their bolts, an explosive light burst out from behind him. The surroundings went pure white.

With the light radiating from behind him, Loren was hardly affected, but the archers taking aim were suddenly showered with it after long hours peering through darkness. They were completely blinded, a few of them even dropping their bows.

<Go, Mister! Go!>

"No need to tell me twice!"

The split-second opening was more than enough for Loren. He cleared the distance to the camp, using his momentum to charge straight into a corner of the gathering.

Once he decided he would do something, Loren knew no hesitation. While he was ashamed to admit it, there were times in his mercenary days when he'd found himself throwing his body and sword at over a hundred enemies. Alone.

Not that he fully trusted Lapis's conviction. The bandits just weren't in perfect fighting form. They were either asleep or partying after the day's plundering, so he figured he'd be able to cut down at least a couple.

Of course, he was completely in the dark about what was going to pull his ass out of the fire after that. Without a plan, he would be surrounded and taken out, but he had to tell himself it would work out somehow.

It wasn't particularly commendable to go with the flow like that, but every mercenary found himself cornered sometimes. Only the ones who could make the most out of a terrible situation survived.

"Wh-who are—gah?!"

With the light—presumably from Lapis—on his side, Loren leapt forward and swung his sword at the first man to stutter out a question.

Loren's foe raised his hands to shield his eyes and failed to put up any defense against an upward slash with all Loren's weight and speed behind it. Loren felt hardly any resistance as his sword bit into the bandit and chewed all the way through.

The damp sound of severed muscle and the hard crunch of bones filled the air while the torso of the bisected bandit spun circles through the sky. The rest of his body slumped to the side, disgorging blood and guts.

That's one down, Loren made the mental tally mark as he pressed forward. His first enemy hadn't had a chance to scream;

the rest of the archers didn't yet grasp their situation. He managed to slip right into the midst of their ranks, swinging his sword in a wide arc.

He caught one in the chin and heaved upward. This one did scream as his face was split in two. Another, Loren managed to sever at the shoulder. As the man lost his balance and fell, Lapis's light dissipated, and Loren was back to relying on the bonfire.

He could see some men flailing their weapons wildly, completely blinded. Others shot arrows into the dark, hollering as they peppered the empty plain with aimless arrows. Loren dispatched the blind, immobile men he'd wounded in his first strike.

"Enemy raid! Enemy raid!"

"You little shit! Where did he crawl out from?!"

The flash and the screams alerted the rest of the camp. Loren knew that much was inevitable, and he didn't panic. He counted up the number of fallen bodies and sent a message to Scena.

"I took out a few of them!"

<*Leave it to me.* Create Undead!>

The powers of a Lifeless King unfurled from within him. A fog so devouringly black that it stood out against the night crept along the ground, hovering over the bodies of the slain bandits before enveloping them completely. The slowly forming black mass slunk over the corpses, letting out an ear-grating rumble.

Loren understood that Scena could turn dead things into zombies and skeletons—but he also knew he was the worst harvester to supply her with the necessary components. Enemies slain by his blade were mercilessly scattered in every direction. How could she make anything useful with that?

She sure proved him wrong. After swallowing the scattered bodies, the mass of creeping darkness coalesced into one heaving whole.

<Not enough, Mister. I can't make anything good. Should I still go ahead?>

"I don't care, just hurry up!"

There was a limit to what a one-man sneak attack could accomplish. Resisting the onset of panic, Loren continued cutting down the mercenaries even as they gathered themselves into proper formation to face him.

Each time one of his heavy blows felled a bandit, the black fog overtook the body and fed it into the black mass. Little by little, with each limb or bit of body, it grew, until Scena finally called out, *<Come to me! Undead Knight!>*

A thick left arm punched out from the mass of darkness. At first glance, it looked human, but it was several times too thick, and its skin had the dried-out, desiccated texture of a mummy's. The sight of it sent a roil of fear through the bandits.

The arm was immediately followed by a torso, then a massive head. The rib cage, little more than skin stretched over a bare skeleton, matched its arm for size. It had a rusted breastplate strapped over its leather and bones. Limbs encased in tarnished armor, faulds, and greaves followed. Last to emerge was a right hand gripping a rust-red halberd.

Loren was quite large himself, but even he had to look up to take in the bulk of Scena's undead knight. The surrounding bandits froze, petrified by the sheer intensity of its massive halberd. The summoned creature unleashed a roar into the night sky so great that the ground shook beneath it. Like lightning, it lashed out with its weapon.

That corroded blade didn't look fit to cut anything, yet by virtue of its wielder's strength, it tore straight through the bodies of the bandits standing dumbly before it. Their husks flew into the sky.

The undead knight moved as casually as a farmer harvesting wheat with his scythe, yet each swing inevitably claimed multiple lives. The scene was a complete nightmare. Loren couldn't help but stop and stare, his sword arm stilled.

"You call that 'nothing good'?" he asked.

<You would be able to beat it pretty easily, Mister.>

"I don't want to fight something like that..."

Without paying the slightest mind to defense, the undead knight recklessly swung its halberd at any enemy that was unlucky enough to catch its attention. Naturally, the bandits rallied themselves to counterattack. It was peppered with arrows while heavily armored fighters closed in and beat at it with their weapons.

Those weapons did have some effect—the arrows pierced through flesh, the blades sliced off bits of bone—but the undead knight ignored all this entirely, swinging its halberd without flinching or yielding. The undead had no sense of pain or fatigue; it would continue fulfilling its purpose until completely destroyed or exorcised.

"You really think I could take that?"

< You could do it. You're strong. But I'm not calling just one of them, so even you might be in trouble. >

As if to punctuate her words, the dark fog swallowed up the bandits slain by Scena's first summon. It swelled up once more as a black amalgamation, and a second undead knight appeared.

"This is getting out of hand," Loren said.

He wasn't keeping a precise count, and he didn't know how many he had defeated, but Loren knew he couldn't match the speed and efficiency of the undead knights. He leaned his sword against his shoulder and watched. The bandits were already helpless against the slaughter wrought by one undead foe, and now it had a buddy.

The killing went twice as fast, piling up twice as many corpses, and it wasn't long before a third and fourth undead knight were born.

"The hell are these things?!"

"It's hopeless! Our attacks aren't working!"

"Run away! It's stupid to take on these monsters!"

When the fourth one joined the party, the bandits lost all morale. Their attacks were technically working, but the massive undead shrugged off any damage. And so, terror-stricken, the bandits scattered in all directions like baby spiders under a boot. The moment she saw this, Scena created something new.

< Come to me! Zombie Dog! >

A zombie dog, it seemed, required fewer bodies than an undead knight. Scena's call was answered swiftly. Several half-rotten dogs emerged from her fog, jumping at the backs of the fleeing bandits to cut them off.

"Dammit! What are they?! Where are they coming from?!"

Perhaps because they were easier to summon, the dogs could be halved by a bandit's sword or crushed by heavy blows. Unfortunately for the bandits, the rate at which the dogs were created greatly exceeded the rate at which they were destroyed. A bandit who fell in the commotion had his windpipe bitten through. Another had his stomach gouged out, his organs snapped up as a feast for multiple dogs.

<I won't let a single one of them get away! Keep at it until they're gone! It's a slaughter! They shall regret ever being born just to die as dog food!>

Scena's jolly laughter echoed in a corner of Loren's mind. He turned his pale face up to the sky and muttered, "Whoa... This is the first time I ever thought you were scary. And wait, why can you use humans as ingredients to make dogs? Someone explain that to me."

<That's a good question,> Scena mused, then scrambled to smooth over Loren's hollow stare of disbelief. *<No, I mean, well, I just got a little excited, that's all! I'm not a scary girl! I swear!>*

It was a bit late for such protestations.

The camp watch beacons toppled over, igniting their tents. At the edge of the growing firelight, the undead knights were still hard at work turning humans into lumps of flesh. Nearby, the zombie dogs gnawed on the viscera of screaming bandits. What had once been a campsite was now the spitting image of hell.

The only thing Loren had done was cut down the first ten or so bandits. The resulting carnage was remarkably self-sufficient.

The bandit crew had been too bloated, too fattened on its own spoils, for one party to hunt. Loren had thought slicing off even enough to split up the group would be optimistic. But now almost every soul out of two hundred was rust on the halberds or food for the dogs. It was such a mess, he couldn't even figure out if any of them had been lucky enough to scramble away.

"What is this? How does this even happen?"

"It is a valid tactic that only works at night, and only against those outside the realm of the law."

Lapis was beside him before he knew it. Loren turned a doubtful eye toward her, and she looked somewhat hurt by this.

"Don't look at me like I'm some sort of monster," she said sullenly.

"After seeing that, anyone and everyone looks like a monster to me."

From his initial attack to the bandits' total annihilation—as far as Loren was concerned, it had all happened in the blink of an eye. Until just a minute ago, the brigade had been so large it would have taken an army to deal with. Not even a scrap of that strength remained. All he saw were fleeing men being sliced, dragged, and bitten to death. They screamed, pleading for help as they were devoured with relish.

"They got what they deserved. I see no room for sympathy."

"Even so, I sympathize with them just a little bit..."

Loren didn't endorse their actions, not in the slightest. In fact, if these brigands were captured, tried, and hanged the normal way, he wouldn't feel a thing. However, he wasn't sure anyone's crime was bad enough to warrant being swarmed by the undead and slaughtered without warning or a chance to fight back.

"May your sinning souls be reborn as good boys and girls in the next life," Lapis prayed. "Now then, Mr. Loren. Once this calms down, let's retire the undead and look for some nice loot."

"When it comes to being blackhearted, I'd say you really give them a run for their money, Lapis."

"What are you talking about? I'll have you know my chest is white as snow. What part of it is the least bit black? Wait, Mr. Loren? Quit turning away—look at me! Hey!"

"Shut up! Why are you lifting up your clothes? Calm down! Let go of me!"

Lapis ignored the screams of agony rising around them, determined to wrench Loren's head around to look at her. Loren struggled to escape from her demonic grasp.

Realizing she had been excluded, or rather, temporarily forgotten, Scena ordered her undead to search the area, then kicked back for a break in Loren's astral body until one of them remembered her.

"Now then, now then, it's time for our fun looting session," Lapis said with a cheerful smile. By contrast, Loren looked as downtrodden as ever as he scanned the former camp.

It was still night, and their surroundings were dark, but the beacons and cooking pots toppled by Scena's undead still burned, merry flames among the tents. Loren had a decent view.

A decent view of a miserable sight.

All that aside, though, the number of corpses was surprisingly low. Most of the flesh had either been collected as material to summon undead or ended up in an undead dog's stomach. There was nothing to be done about the blood splatters, but this was quite tame, considering the circumstances.

Unconcerned, the undead knights patrolled the area while the zombie dogs ran about looking for any survivors.

"What do we do about this?" Loren muttered.

The number of undead Scena had summoned could easily surround and obliterate a small settlement. Loren understood they'd needed the help to deal with a small legion of bandits, but maybe they'd just replaced a bandit brigade with an undead one. He had a sinking feeling about which one was the bigger threat.

"Weren't we just supposed to rough them up a bit so they'd be forced to split?" he asked.

"I'm surprised by how well it all turned out," Lapis said.

Scena's voice reverberated in his mind. <*It's all right, Mister.*>

Lapis couldn't hear how incredibly cheerful Scena was being in her attempts to alleviate Loren's anxieties.

<*The children I made will disappear come morning.*>

Scena happily explained that she had skipped over some of the proper procedures to so quickly assemble the numbers required. Her hulking, rotting children would return to dust once time or sunlight wore the magic away.

The army of the undead, so suddenly summoned up in the dead of night, weren't about to go on any rampages through the surrounding settlements.

"They're really gonna disappear?"

It was hard to believe such a powerful force could just up and vanish. They still looked pretty energetic to Loren, and he had a sinking feeling that it would be impossible for him to dispatch all of them alone.

"Not that having them disappear will solve all our problems," he murmured.

"Oh?" Lapis asked. "What other problems are there?"

"According to Scena, these guys will disappear at sunrise. When that happens, no one's gonna believe us when we tell them what happened here."

"Huh? What are you talking about?"

The bloodstains smeared across the grass, tents, and every other surface made it obvious that many people had died painfully in this place. If the perpetrators disappeared into sunbeams, that left Loren and Lapis holding the bag with no explanation.

To Loren, it was only natural that step two of this process was reporting the bandit extermination to the guild. But Lapis stared at him as if she didn't understand a single word coming out of his mouth.

"Well, don't we have some obligation to report what happened to them? Or some government official or something? A whole rest town was overrun. A lot of people died."

"That's strange. What exactly are you saying happened here?" Lapis asked, playing dumb. Loren was ready call her out on it, but he shut his mouth when he realized what she had in mind.

It can't be. He stared at her, unable to tear himself away.

She pulled off genuine confusion pretty well, shaking her head and folding her hands in front of her chest.

"What a tragedy it is! I have no doubt in my mind that countless lives ended here, but I haven't the slightest clue what could have caused it. Even if we wanted to determine the terrible cause, we have things to do and places to be. Let us pinch only what the dead no longer need and leave the investigation to someone more suited to the task."

"We're really doing this?"

"Whatever could you be talking about, Mr. Loren?"

<What's she talking about?>

Scena, at least, seemed honestly confused. Loren scowled and explained: in a nutshell, Lapis intended to pretend that she didn't know how or why the town had been attacked, nor why someone had set up a large camp nearby, nor even why the camp had been annihilated by undead—or whatever.

<Will they believe that?>

"There're no witnesses or evidence..."

The rest town had certainly been destroyed by the bandits, and most of the townsfolk reduced to ash along with it. The bandits at fault had subsequently been killed by undead and harvested to make even more undead.

<It's true. There are no witnesses!>

"As long as we keep our mouths shut, the truth will be left in darkness... Though you might want to sew my lips shut, just in case."

"How scary, Mr. Loren. More importantly, you should get to searching already. We need to take what we can and get out of here."

Lapis could casually blurt out the cruelest things. Unfortunately, there was some sense to her barbarism. Loren sighed as he let her beckon him through the campsite. The bandit camp wasn't far from the town, and the town was—had been—a place for travelers to rest their weary heads. Eventually, someone else would make the long trek out.

And what if that someone found the charred remains of the town? If they turned back, whatever. But any decently skilled adventurer might try to gather information before they returned to civilization. And that search would lead them straight to the scattered bodies of the bandits, which in turn could lead them right to Loren and Lapis, whereupon of course they would demand an explanation—one Loren did not want to give, especially not while the undead were still kicking around.

What could he possibly say? That they had employed a Lifeless King to destroy the bandits? If he trotted that one out, they'd be the next bounty on the guild's list.

Despite the chaos, Lapis had put some thought into their troubles. Or so Loren assumed, until she came at it from a completely different angle.

"If anyone else comes," she said, "it means we'll have to split our spoils."

"You're even more of a bandit than they were."

"What are you saying?! I'm simply proposing that we collect valuables from this campsite where everyone mysteriously disappeared."

How shameless can you be? Loren thought, but he wasn't keen on sharing either. All this loot had originally belonged to victims whose names he didn't even know, sure, but it was the bandits who'd stripped everything from the town. Any rightful owners were dead. He couldn't exactly give any of it back. That being the case, they might as well put it to good use.

"Food and clothes will take up too much space," said Lapis. "If they ended up with any captives, young girls, or the like, you can't take them with you."

"I won't."

"Good. We're aiming for jewelry and precious metals. Hard cash if they have it, but you can ignore the copper coins. Too much weight, too little value."

"Your inner bandit is peeking through again."

They kicked their way through the smoldering tents, fishing through whatever was still intact. Bandits or not, the whole organization had needed food, clothing, and daily bric-a-brac—indispensable to the bandits, maybe, but nothing worth it for Loren and Lapis to haul around.

"They shook down an isolated rest town. I doubt we're going to find many precious metals."

Bandits might have craved jewelry and ornaments, things easily melted down and exchanged for cash or barter, but to farmers and other simple folk who lived in such towns, baubles didn't put food on the table. They didn't have means or reason to purchase such pointless things.

As proof of this, Lapis found little in the way of worthy plunder as she searched through tent after tent. No milkmaid or blacksmith made a habit of dressing up, so Loren didn't know what she expected. She didn't try to hide her disappointment.

"Shouldn't they at least have some money?" she complained.

"I mean, we should find a bit of it."

Not that Loren had high hopes for that either. If no one in town was buying or selling valuables, most coins in circulation would have been copper or silver. There just wouldn't have been the sort of wheeling and dealing that required fistfuls of gold.

In short, the bandit brigade had mostly made off with food, ordinary goods, and copper coins. It was possible they'd been after the people more than anything.

If abduction had been the aim, Loren doubted they'd find any hostages. Scena's undead recognized Loren and Lapis and let them be. However, it was hard to believe they'd be willing or able to distinguish between bandits and poor townsfolk.

"Wow. This one is filled with copper coins. Is it really worth the effort to carry this much spare change?"

Lapis finally found the money stash she was looking for, but Loren had expected this outcome. Sure, a bandit had to take what they could get, living from mark to mark. But he could hardly expect Lapis to load so much copper on the donkey. *She's not really taking it, is she?*

An excited shout broke through his thoughts. "Mr. Loren! Have a look at this!"

"What is it? What's exciting enough that you had to yell about it?"

He walked over to where Lapis was rummaging through her

umpteenth tent and had stopped to point at something. His eyes fell upon it.

It was a large box. At first, he would have guessed it contained clothing. However, Lapis had thrown open the lid to reveal nothing of the sort. Well, it did contain clothing after a fashion, but those clothes were being worn by an unconscious person curled into a tight ball.

Blond hair just brushing slim shoulders. Near-translucent white skin, and a plain green top and breeches. Probably a preteen. Their strange, fine features made it difficult to discern whether they were a boy or girl. Unfortunately, their beauty made obvious why the bandits had taken them.

What surprised Loren the most were the child's ears. Like those of an archer they had once met in a silver-ranked party, the child's ears were long and slender.

"An elf?"

"Looks like it. This is smelling like trouble again."

They couldn't just close the box and pretend they hadn't seen anything, but toting a kidnapped child around was asking for trouble.

Loren looked to the heavens. *Why did it have to be here of all places?* he complained.

All the while, Lapis looked at him with a thin smile, just as uncertain.

3 Withdrawal to Relief

Ultimately, their glorious bounty from the bandit camp was one small sack of silver coins, a few cheap decorations, some middling-expensive bottles of wine, and a few food supplies.

That was far too little reward for the effort put in, Lapis complained, but Loren didn't know what effort she was taking credit for. Rather, on the topic of effort, he got the feeling there was a lot more of that to come. The likelihood of that was as evident as the elf child slung over their donkey's neck.

A child in looks, at least, but Loren figured the elf might be far older than he appeared. According to Lapis, though, elves grew at the same rate as humans up to a certain age. After that, their appearances stopped changing, and they lived for many years as young men and women. Apparently it was safe to assume any elf from childhood through adolescence was about as old as they looked.

On the other side of the spectrum were elves who, no matter how young and beautiful they looked, were over ten times his age.

Lapis insisted Loren must keep this in mind if he ever tried hitting on them.

Now Loren didn't know if he was ever going to hit on an elf, but he filed that one away regardless.

"Still, what was the kid doing in a box?" Loren muttered as he led the donkey by its lead. Lapis couldn't give him answer. There were riddles that even a priest to the god of knowledge couldn't solve.

Loren was prepared to live with the riddle of whether the child was a boy or girl, but Lapis was easily able to make the distinction. Once Loren had carried the child out of the camp to where he had tethered the donkey, Lapis grabbed him by the wrist and shoved his hand into the child's crotch.

"How is it feeling?" She didn't seem bothered at all after casually doing something so terrible.

"You little..." Loren had to contain himself from cursing at her. "He's a boy."

"Oh, a boy then. That leaves the question of why the bandits would go out of their way to confine an elf boy in such a way... Well, everyone has their own tastes. I can't say there isn't a demand for that sort of thing."

"Don't just do something like that. Luckily, he's a boy, so I get ticked and that's the end of the story. What were you gonna do if he was a girl?" Loren said with a sour face. He was still reeling from the psychological damage he could have inflicted had the child been a girl, let alone remotely conscious.

"Let's just say you were lucky."

"To hell with that, you vile demon!"

Use your own hand next time, thought Loren. Although a beautiful woman shoving her hand into a little girl or boy's crotch didn't conjure up images of a better scenario on the whole. Ultimately, the only victims were himself and an unconscious child who'd have no memory of the incident. He told himself it was better that way.

Mister's getting stained by the missus, thought Scena, but she made sure those words didn't reach her host.

"So what do we do about him?" Loren asked.

They started moving before daybreak. Lapis thought they would be at risk of someone spotting them if they lingered, and Loren couldn't argue. He was feeling far too guilty; if someone questioned them, he'd spill the beans about the whole fiasco. Lapis could easily pretend she didn't know a thing, but Loren wasn't so skillful with his words.

"I did consider leaving him there," said Lapis.

Behind them, Scena's summoned undead remained stationed around the camp. They would stay there until their final moments, if Scena was to be believed. If the elf boy were left with them, they would promptly devour him.

Loren believed that it was within Lapis's moral capacity to choose that option. That she hadn't meant she had something else in mind. When Loren asked her, though, her answers were steadfastly unclear.

"I just have this vague notion. It bothered me that we ran across an elf right on our way to a forest with elven settlements."

"Acting on a hunch?"

"Well, something like that."

"You won't be cursed by the entire elven race if you kill an elf or something, right?"

"Even if that were true, it would be the undead who got cursed."

This was by no means a justification, to Loren's mind.

Lapis looked down at the elf boy. "I don't know what the circumstances are, but it's hard to believe this child was in that box of his own volition. I can only think he was kidnapped. I'm sure his family is worried about him."

"You could get a sob story out of it, I guess."

It was possible she was acting out of pure self-interest. Surely the elves would give them a warm welcome if they returned a missing child to his family's loving embrace. Even so, there was nothing objectional about the plan. Loren patted his chest in relief, certain Lapis wasn't devious enough to use the boy as bait to lure other elves out for catching and selling.

He didn't know how the bandits had managed to capture the elf child, but that they'd dragged him all the way out here meant they likely intended to sell him. Good-looking elves fetched quite a hefty price; elves a tad older would go for even more.

"By the look on your face, you must be imagining something dreadful," Lapis told him.

"Have a good look in the mirror someday."

"Even I wouldn't even think about using the boy to sniff out their hideout, pretending we'd saved him so we could infiltrate and capture their entire settlement! Not in the slightest!"

"So you *were* thinking about it."

What's more, her imagination was even worse than his. She waved her hands in the air, shooing it all off as a joke.

They carried on conversing as they continued their route parallel to the highway.

The elven boy finally awoke when a sliver of the sun peeked over the horizon. He rocked back and forth on the donkey's back as he opened his eyes, rubbing the sleep from them. Then he started screaming.

"Hmm? Did you just hear a really shrill shriek?" Loren asked.

He stood before a handful of dead ogres, all sitting cross-legged and quite dead on the ground. After all, their original goal in journeying out here had been to collect monster parts and sell them to the guild at Kaffa. They'd found these ogres shortly before the elf boy awakened—a clan of giant man-eating orcs from who knew where.

Ogres were several times stronger than a fully grown human, and their blows, while sloppy, were incredibly powerful. Even shields and armor did little to protect against their might.

Any run-of-the-mill copper-rank adventuring party would have said their last prayers if they encountered more than one ogre. With sufficient numbers, they could make even an iron-rank party struggle.

There were around ten corpses in total. This was far more than a mere copper-rank should have been able to handle, but Loren and Lapis had dealt with them without suffering so much as a bruise.

The boy awakened just as they were busy cutting off the monstrous bits that would prove their kills.

"Oh? Did a traveler see us?" Lapis lifted her face, her hands bright red with blood from slicing horns and fangs off the lifeless bodies. She was surrounded by these bloodstained spoils, a merciless butcher. Some of the ogre bodies were completely covered in gore.

At the sight, the elf boy screamed again and toppled from the donkey, shuffling back, attempting to crawl his way to freedom.

"Hey, where do you think you're running to?" Lapis demanded.

She quickly closed in on him, pinning him down with a foot on his back. She didn't intend any cruelty by this; she had rolled up her sleeves to work, and she was covered in blood from her fingertips to her elbows. She couldn't bring herself to grab him with her hands.

Yet from an outside perspective, there it was: a bloodstained girl stomping down upon a crying child trying desperately to crawl away. It was so appalling that Loren stopped his own dismantling duties and reached out to help the boy. Naturally, his hands were just as streaked with gore. The boy's screams reached a more furious pitch.

"You're making too much noise." She leaned into the kid a bit harder.

Even that bit of pressure was enough to make the boy yelp as he kicked and squirmed to get free. The poor thing's efforts didn't bear any fruit, and after a bit of thrashing, he slumped in resignation.

"Mr. Loren, would you wash your hands, and look after the kid? I'll continue the dismantling work."

Loren doused his hands with water from the waterskin they'd set aside, then shook away the droplets. Suitably dry, Loren carefully removed Lapis's foot, then lifted the boy up and placed him back on the donkey.

"Don't be so scared. We saved you, for what it's worth. You can at least remember who abducted you and how you were treated, right?" Loren said, but he wasn't sure if the kid could even understand him.

That silver-ranked elf, Nym, knew the human tongue well enough to converse, but elves had their own languages. He remembered hearing stories about those who didn't wander into human settlements because they found humans impossible to communicate with.

So which is it with this one? Loren wondered. While the elf boy had started out tense, now the difference between his current circumstances and the ones he'd faced before he lost consciousness seemed to dawn on him. The fear drained slowly from his face, and Loren let out a sigh of relief.

"You...saved me?"

Loren hesitated. How should he answer that? If he said no, the boy would go right back to being terrified. However, Loren could hardly say yes when he didn't know what Lapis was planning for the kid. He glanced over at her where she'd gotten right back to the dismembering work; she must have noticed him staring, but she didn't look up. Her hands didn't stop, she just offered a little nod.

It was up to him, apparently. In the time it'd taken to do that mental math, his silence had already made the boy anxious.

"Yeah, we saved you. You were captured by bandits, and we got you out of there. I'm Loren, and that priest over there is named Lapis. We're headed for the Black Forest. Is that where you're from?"

If the kid wasn't from the Black Forest, they'd be in for even more trouble.

The elf nodded. "That's what humankind called the forest I was in. I heard it from a peddler who stopped by."

So the boy's settlement had some trade with humans, and he spoke the human tongue without issue. Maybe everything would work itself out. Even as she worked, Loren knew Lapis's ears were homed in on their conversation, so he spoke on to draw out as much useful information as he could.

The boy introduced himself as Feuille, and it took nearly half a day to pluck out all the details Loren wanted.

At first, it was a trial and a half just to get a name out of him. Perhaps because Feuille was young, there were times where he didn't quite understand Loren's questions, or other times when his memory would lapse or scramble. As Loren listened to the kid ramble, everything started going in one ear and out the other.

Luckily, Lapis and her eavesdropping got all the facts tidied up into logical order. By the time Feuille fell back to sleep on the donkey's back, she had a good grasp on the situation.

Apparently, Feuille was an elf who lived in one of the settlements within the Black Forest, and he was ten years old. He had been helping his friends gather fruit and medicinal herbs when they made a mistake and wandered past the forest's borders. Unfortunately, this misadventure culminated in them being chased by multiple ill-mannered men.

The men managed to round up all the elven children and tried to lead them away. However, the brigands fumbled this job so badly that many children were killed, and nearly all the others managed to escape. Ultimately, their only captive was Feuille, who had tripped and twisted his ankle.

With his arms and legs tied, the men carried him for about a day, ending up back at their camp, where they stuffed him into the box Lapis eventually found him in. Feuille, of course, was worried about what would become of him. He'd cried himself out and fallen asleep, and he didn't remember a thing after that.

Loren couldn't tell whether the kid was lucky or not. Still, since he had been unconscious in a box at the time, he hadn't seen the undead, and his life had been spared, it was hard to call him *un*lucky.

"We didn't even learn anything interesting," Lapis complained as she stared at the sleeping boy.

As far as the kid was concerned, his story was a series of close calls between life and death. Loren failed to see where being interesting was supposed to factor in.

When he told Lapis it would be dangerous to enter the Black Forest with Feuille in tow, she looked at him quizzically.

"Why would we be in danger?" she asked.

"The other kids were murdered. The elves might think we're in cahoots with their kidnappers."

"Would a kidnapper come straight back to hand over a child?"

"Maybe not."

Rationally speaking, she was right, but misunderstandings made their own mischief. It wasn't outside the realm of possibility that the elves would hear of a human bringing a captured child back, only to conclude that the culprit had returned.

"And it's elves we're dealing with here," Loren added.

"Yes, well, I suppose it's possible."

Even if the elves didn't pin the crime on Loren and Lapis, they might assume they were part of a ploy to use Feuille to infiltrate the settlement. Or that the boy had been brought home solely for the reward. There were more than a few possibilities, and not a lot of them involved someone delivering a wayward child home completely out of the goodness of their heart.

"The elves do have their share of weirdoes."

"I'm sure even the elves wouldn't want to hear that from a demon."

Lapis went sullen at this biting remark but could offer no rebuttal. Sniping at each other about their potential murder-by-elf, they traveled the rest of the day without incident. By evening, they had reached the town closest to the Black Forest.

By sheer coincidence, the town had a branch office of the adventurers' guild.

"It seems I was a bit lacking in information," said Lapis. "I didn't expect such convenience."

Before even booking an inn, they headed over to turn in their monster parts. When Feuille regained consciousness, they had been butchering ten ogres, but they'd taken out a few monsters while he napped as well.

This resulted in quite a lot to carry. They were better off dealing with it before they headed into the forest.

"What do you mean, you're not going to pay us?"

The receptionist's smile didn't waver as she took the ominous, bloody sack Loren had dumped on her counter. She shook her head. "I'm afraid not. At this location, we only have the facilities to assess and store your spoils. We can issue a written certificate, so please turn it in at your base guild to receive your money."

"I see."

It was a hassle, and no doubt Loren would be anxious about his pay for the entire trip back, but at least he could lighten their load. Even better, the branch office was attached to a bar just like the guild in Kaffa.

Loren cocked a thumb at Feuille, who stood fidgeting behind him. "I'll take care of things here. Go feed him something. I doubt he's eaten anything good for a while now."

Captured, tied up, and sealed away, it was hard to imagine Feuille had received any proper care. It was hard for a young child to skip even a single meal, so Lapis nodded and walked Feuille to the bar. The bar served food as well as alcohol, and Loren was sure a child would be allowed in.

As he turned, the contents of his sack were spread out across the counter, and the receptionist paused in her assessment to raise a dubious eyebrow at their retreating backs.

"Something catch your eye?" he asked her, casual enough to invite idle gossip.

The receptionist, caught staring at her client's comrades, hung her head in shame but nodded.

Are elves that rare in these parts? Loren wondered. The town was right next to the Black Forest where elves were known to live, and those elves traded with human settlements. It would be strange for an elf to be worth staring at.

"My travel partner?" Loren guessed. "Sure, she's young and pretty. I'm sure she could've become whatever she wanted, but she chose to be a priest."

But the receptionist shook her head. That wasn't what had drawn her eye. "Your companion is beautiful...but, and I don't mean to be rude, you have an elven child with you... And I just couldn't help but look."

She lowered her head, and he waved his hand to say he didn't mind. The thing he'd doubted was true; he needed to dig to find out why.

"This town is right next to the Black Forest, right? Aren't you used to seeing elves?"

"Yes, it was like that until a short while ago."

That was rather ominous. If elves had been frequently spotted before, what had happened more recently? Had they all vanished?

"Well, I wouldn't say frequently," she said when he asked. "But they would stop by from time to time to trade their wood carvings and fruit."

"And you're saying that all stopped?"

"Not only that. The people who trade with the elves grew worried, so they hired some guards and ventured into the forest."

The receptionist covered her mouth and beckoned him closer. What came next wasn't to be made public. She placed her mouth close to his ear and whispered, "Not a single one has come back. It's been a few days now, though the Black Forest is so vast that they might still be investigating."

The receptionist didn't pause in her work as they gossiped. She tallied up each monster part, sorting them into different subdivisions, and wrote quantities and estimated values on a slip of paper.

"If they don't come back soon, we'll have to post a quest for a search party," she went on. "We're only a small branch office, and we don't have much money to spare. First, we'll need to seek help from the nearby guilds."

"Sounds worrying."

"My thoughts exactly. All the way out here, there aren't too many adventurers we can count on. Too few regulars at such a tiny branch office. It would be incredibly helpful if a well-meaning adventurer checked in on the situation." She glanced up at Loren.

He answered with a wry smile.

A two-person party had brought in the bounty of ten ogres; that was more than enough to declare them competent. As far as ranks were concerned, they were mere copper, but those numbers were beyond the capabilities of your typical coppers.

As far as Loren was concerned, though, he wasn't interested in fulfilling the duty the receptionist wanted to heap upon him. He had absolutely no intention of working for free.

"You might get some takers if you put out a quest," he said.

"We won't know how much money to offer until we have a clearer grasp of the situation."

"So it's an investigation into launching an investigation. Well, if I feel up to it and there's money involved, I wouldn't mind giving you a hand, but I've got a partner to consider. I can't decide on my own."

"You have a point. All right, I've finished your assessment. Here's your certificate." The receptionist let the conversation end there, her request casual and curious. She scrawled her signature at the bottom of their monster-harvest receipt.

Loren said his thanks as he took it. But as he turned to head back to Lapis, the receptionist whispered at his back.

"How about I make it a little worth your while?"

He turned to see her smiling and pointing at the board where all the quests were posted. He squinted his eyes to make sure he hadn't missed her posting, but it seemed she was going to put it up soon.

"I'll be counting on it," he told her, acting as though it was none of his concern.

When he found Lapis, Feuille was stuffing his face with stew, bread, and greens. Lapis sat smiling at the kid.

"Welcome back. How was it?"

Loren knew she didn't care much about the assessment sheet, but he handed it over anyway. She took it without a word, scanned it, and tucked it away.

"Very well." Her tone demanded he present something more

intriguing. He pulled out a chair, sat down, and detailed his conversation with the receptionist.

They had to book a room at the inn for the night, and Loren hesitated over how to handle Feuille. Booking three rooms, one for each of them, would be costly, but at first it seemed like the obvious answer. Then he began to doubt the wisdom of leaving Feuille on his own.

Feuille might have been an elf, but he was still only ten years old; it didn't seem like a good idea to leave a child alone. But when he suggested having the boy stay with him, he felt the daggers of harsh glares stabbing between his shoulder blades.

He turned to meet a wave of mean looks from the customers crammed into the inn's dining area. He knew this wasn't hostility or malice—he felt enough of those on the battlefield to recognize them. Then what could it be? Loren didn't have a clue, but it likely had something to do with how the eyes of the lady adventurers were especially cold.

Lapis stroked him on the nape and whispered, "I'm assuming here...but could it be that they think that Mr. Feuille is a girl?"

He looked down at the boy beside him. Elves usually had fine features—both the men and the women—but Feuille was especially delicate-looking and androgynous. It would be hard to identify his gender at a glance, and even after a long hard stare, some would conclude he was a girl.

Point being, it looked like Loren was trying to lead a little girl to his room. Once he realized that, he tried shoving the kid off onto Lapis, but she wasn't having it.

"Appearances aside, Mr. Feuille is a boy."

"Yeah, so?"

"You want a pure, unmarried maiden such as myself to spend the night with a man?!"

"Ah, right."

"What was that pause for?"

Lapis tried kicking up a fuss, but Loren ignored her and started reviewing his options. Keeping Feuille in his own room would upset the other patrons. Lapis didn't want to look after the kid, which left only one solution.

"How about one large room for the three of us?" he asked.

"What, are you a family or something?" the owner of the inn—a middle-aged man—piped up.

Loren considered this would-be family structure: a human, a demon, and an elf. That would really be quite the mess.

"Not exactly. It's difficult to explain. I'd appreciate if you didn't pry into it."

"We have one large room up for rent that fits five. It's three silver upfront for a night, with two meals included. You have to pay extra if you want more towels and hot water."

It seemed the owner was trying to be considerate to their not-exactly-family situation, but this heaped more stress onto Loren's plate. He pulled an exhausted face as he slid three silver coins across the table. That put a dent in the few silver coins he had left in his wallet. But it would have tarnished his image even further to have Lapis pay for it, so he put up the money before she could.

The owner checked the coins, then slid a key into Loren's hand and gave him some directions.

This is costing more than I'd hoped, Loren thought as he led Lapis and Feuille to the second floor and into the large room. Loren lowered his bag and weapon in a corner, sat on the bed, and took a deep breath before he finally noticed Feuille was looking at him.

"What's wrong?" he called out, as the boy was standing stock-still in the doorway.

There was concern on the boy's face as he asked, "Umm...what's going to happen to me?"

The question was vague. Lacking an answer for him, Loren turned to Lapis. She had also lowered her luggage and sat on a separate bed. Once she noticed Loren's gaze, she placed her index finger to her chin, letting her gaze prowl the ceiling. She spoke hesitantly.

"Going about it the orthodox way would mean dragging you with us through the Black Forest to deliver you back to your people."

"That sounds about right, but what do you mean orthodox? You mean there's some other way?" Loren asked.

"Do you want to hear it?"

"If you don't want me to hear it, don't bring it up in the first place."

There was no telling what Lapis might come up with. Loren ignored her for the time being and turned back to Feuille in the doorway.

"If you've got some way of contacting your family, we can go with that," he said. "Otherwise, you'll have to guide us to your settlement. Sure, you're an elf, but I don't want to let a kid hike through the Black Forest alone."

The moment Loren mentioned being guided to the settlement, Feuille tensed up, hesitant. Loren knew he should have phrased it better, perhaps as them guarding Feuille on the way home. Lapis glared at him, her smile a bitter twist.

The elves were a fair race, so fair that many scoundrels were out for their bodies. From the boy's reaction, Loren could tell he'd seen his share of troubles.

"I don't have any business with your settlement," he said. "I just want to get you there properly."

"Are you sure?" Feuille asked. "I don't have any money to pay you."

From their visit to the guild, Feuille must have picked up that they were adventurers. It would make perfect sense for adventurers to demand payment for taking Feuille home.

"Don't worry, I never expected any money out of you."

"Th-then my parents..."

I see, Loren thought. It would not be commendable to squeeze money out of a small child, but anyone could justify bringing a lost child home and expecting payment from the relatives.

Loren shook the thought from his head. "I didn't take on a job to deliver a lost child home."

"In that case..."

"The ship has sailed, as they say. There must be some reason we picked you up. We'll deliver you home free of charge, and we won't demand payment for the room either. Don't worry."

"Why are you going so far...?"

It was, apparently, incredibly rare to find an adventurer who would do so much for a stranger without any reward. Feuille seemed to find the whole idea absurd. Loren wondered what he could say to convince the boy, but he realized he had no obligation to be convincing.

Feuille could accept the proposal or turn it down at no cost whatsoever. Even if they parted right at the entrance to the forest, Loren wouldn't be any worse off. In fact, that would be a lot less trouble for him—other than the trouble of many sleepless nights after setting a defenseless child loose in the Black Forest, which was a punishment Loren preferred to avoid.

"I don't have a reason. I guess, if anything..."

"It's because Mr. Loren here is nice to a fault," Lapis interjected, cutting Loren off.

Who's nice to a fault? Loren wanted to demand, but he could see how his logic might come off that way. He fell silent when Lapis stared at him.

"So why not take us up on that for now?" Lapis asked. "After you're home safe, you can give us whatever payment you like, if you really want. That's how I'm looking at it."

"R-really?"

Assured by Lapis's kind words, Feuille finally moved from his spot to the last empty bed. It was supposed to be a room for five, but Loren noted two long sofas that had apparently been included in the count. They had lucked into exactly enough beds.

Lapis interrupted his assessment of the room. "All right, Mr. Loren," she declared as if she had only just remembered. "Then all that's left is to eat, sleep, and enter the Black Forest tomorrow."

"Okay, and so?"

"Well, did the man not say that hot water and towels were an additional fee? I'd like to freshen myself up before bed." She let out a pronounced sigh. "What terrible, miserly service."

Loren thought back to his conversation with the innkeeper. "No, he only said *more* towels. The lodging fee should include enough to get ourselves wiped down."

Loren didn't think he was remembering wrong, but Lapis looked rather vexed as she continued to press him.

"Does that mean he's not going to prepare enough for us to get properly clean?"

That probably ain't it, thought Loren. Even the cheapest inns he stayed at gave him enough water and a spare cloth to wipe himself down. Given that they were renting a five-person room for only three people, the staff couldn't complain if they asked for enough water and towels for five. It was difficult to imagine that not being enough.

The only real hiccup was that Loren and Feuille would have to leave the room while Lapis washed, though that was hardly an issue.

"I don't need much myself, and I doubt Feuille does either. We should get enough for five, and you can use whatever's left, Lapis."

"I see, I won't say I'm not grateful... But then why did the owner bring it up?"

"Who knows? Maybe they get clients that use a stupid amount of towels and water? Or maybe he just wanted to make sure we knew the rules?"

Loren tried to play it off. He didn't want to say it out loud, but he did fully understand why the owner had brought up the water and towels. The innkeeper anticipated a mess because Loren was leading along a girl like Lapis, and Feuille who looked like a girl, and neither of them were family.

Loren thought Lapis would be able to solve the riddle without him having to spell it out for her, but it seemed she just didn't get it. Maybe this was an issue stemming from demonic bathing culture. If three unrelated people ever needed more water and towels, they could just hop in the bath.

<What does that mean, Mister?> Scena piped up inside his head. <Please explain it to me.>

Loren nearly retorted, "You're ten years too young to know." But Scena, lurking inside him, was the astral body of the highest-ranking form of undead. She wouldn't be an adult in ten years or twenty. A better answer might be "It's too early for you to know." Or maybe "I'll explain when you're an adult"? Loren weighed his options.

<Did I ask something I shouldn't have?> Scena stammered at his hesitation.

Her voice brought him back to his senses. *I'll tell you if I ever feel like it.*

Having successfully dodged the question, he flopped flat on the bed.

4 Camping Out to an Encounter

THE PARTY SET OFF for the Black Forest the next day. The owner of the inn seemed like he had something to say as they headed out, but Loren shut him up with a murderous glare.

Loren didn't usually care about gossip one way or the other, but he didn't like standing back and letting baseless nonsense shred his reputation. Maybe the man found it odd that he hadn't come for those extra towels, but Loren wanted him to understand that a man and woman staying a night in the same room didn't necessarily mean they were getting up to anything...messy.

"Let's restock a bit before we go," Lapis said, oblivious to Loren's predicament.

They couldn't take the borrowed donkey with them, so they left it at the guild branch, and they replenished their stock at a general store nearby.

"I get the feeling my debts are piling up..."

They split the bill on the necessary quest expenses, but everything else came from Lapis's wallet. Anyone watching would have thought she footed the entire bill. Even in the general store, he got cold looks.

"It shouldn't be too much, this time around."

They only bought a few food rations, some salve, tinder, and oil. Having Feuille around meant they needed a bit more than they had planned for, but a kid that small didn't increase their load by much.

"I'll put Mr. Feuille's expenses on your tab," Lapis said.

"Fine, go ahead."

Maybe she would have split that too if he asked. However, Lapis had no such obligation, and Loren accepted responsibility. She looked a little irritated when he didn't complain, but she quickly snapped back to her usual expression. Just as swiftly, she packed up the supplies and tallied the costs.

"Umm... I can pay for myself...once I'm back..."

Loren placed a hand on Feuille's head to cut him off. He ruffled the boy's hair, a vague smile on his face. His large hand engulfed Feuille's small head, and a friendly ruffling turned into a tornado. Feuille's head spun in dizzied circles, and he grabbed onto a nearby shelf to prevent himself from teetering over.

"Quit worrying about that. For now, just focus on getting home. We don't know the way, so we're counting on you to see us through."

"R-right."

"It's not like we're working for nothing. We came to the Black Forest to do a bit of monster hunting. It'd be great if we had the guidance of the ever-knowledgeable elves."

Loren proudly unveiled his reason for saving Feuille—he'd spent the entire night thinking it up. Loren's reasons were his own, and he didn't mind if he was taken as some figure of charitable virtue. Unfortunately, people were often suspicious of any explanation that didn't end in profit. They simply didn't believe in that sort of miracle.

The moment Loren brought up the idea of a return favor, people were relieved—that was how the world worked. However, were he to ask for some great compensation, he would leave a bad impression on Feuille's parents and the other elves of his settlement.

And so, with all of that considered, Loren came up with this idea: he would act as if he banked on getting monster intel from the elves once he was in the settlement. They were undoubtedly the most knowledgeable on the subject, after all. It was just the right amount of greedy without touching anyone's coin purse.

Even if the information they offered wasn't worthwhile, Loren hadn't expected any assistance before rescuing Feuille. If the elves did have some keen insights, that would be a happy bonus.

"You get it now, right?" asked Loren. "So just kick back and let us look after you."

"Thank you."

Whether he understood Loren's full intentions or not, Feuille was grateful. Loren released his head and smiled, only for Lapis to tug at his sleeve.

"What's up?" he asked.

"Don't you think it would be nice to share a bit of that kindness with me sometimes?"

"I think I've been pretty open-minded about your behavior. How do you expect me to be kinder than that?"

In response, Lapis only darted off; Loren wondered if he'd kicked the hornet's nest.

They finished their preparations here and there before eating lunch in town, and then they were off. The tree line of the Black Forest was around half a day's walk from the town. It was an enormous forest. Farther in, the trees grew so densely, they blocked off all sunlight, rendering the wood dark as night. Many different races, elves and others, thrived in small settlements within.

"There are all sorts. Goblins and orcs, for one. Then you've got villages of fairies, then elves like us."

Along the way, Feuille desperately tried explaining the ways of the Black Forest, as if he wanted to shove all of the information into Lapis and Loren before they even saw a tree.

"How are elves and fairies different?" Loren asked.

"The small ones with wings are fairies, and the big ones without wings are elves," Lapis replied. "Rumor has it that they were once one and the same."

<I think I'm pretty fairy-like.> Scena flapped her wings in the corner of Loren's vision. He gazed absentmindedly at the invisible girl as Lapis continued her lecture.

Originally, there had been only spirits, entities that existed as little more than astral bodies. For whatever reason, those spirits decided to take on physical incarnations; the ones that took on humanoid forms were elves, while fairies stuck closer to their original spirit forms.

Both races preferred the natural environment of the forest and detested base metals like iron and copper. They also both tended to be somewhat prideful and were wont to belittle humankind.

Loren thought back to the elven archer he had met before. He hadn't felt she was either haughty or scornful. Moreover, not only had she come to live in human civilization, she seemed get along quite well with the people she found there. Maybe she was a weird elf.

Having left town around noon, they arrived at the outer edge of the forest just before sunset. Loren thought they would enter right then and there, but Lapis suggested they put it off to the next morning. They would spend the night camped on the outskirts.

It was dark enough in the forest as it was, she reasoned. Moving around at night only increased the danger. She had a point, and both Loren and Feuille were convinced.

"It really is pitch black if you go too far in, but my people don't live so deep. It's just a bit dim during the day. We're definitely better off waiting until the sun is high in the sky."

"Do you know the way?"

"Probably... I think it'll be okay."

The forest looked like nothing but identical trees to Loren and Lapis. There weren't any paths through it, but maybe the boy could see something they couldn't. He stared at the forest a bit before nodding confidently.

Looks like it won't be too difficult getting him home. Loren felt a weight lift off his shoulders.

"Well, whatever happens," said Lapis, "it will have to wait until tomorrow. Let's set up camp."

"Is it all right to camp out right next to the forest?" Loren asked.

Near or far, there was nothing but grass and trees, so he didn't think it made much of a difference. But if some monster did come trying to eat them, it would likely burst out of the tree line. It was probably safer to distance themselves a bit.

Lapis stared back at the plains for a minute. "If we want to gather firewood and stave off the wind, I believe it would be more convenient to remain near the forest. The wind will grow harsh if we're too far away."

They hadn't brought any firewood with them. Adventurers didn't bother purchasing and carrying what they could scavenge along the way. And Lapis had a point—the wind sweeping over the plains was bitingly cold, and even their tents couldn't offer them total shelter from it. Thus, Lapis was of a mind to use the trees as a windbreak and keep near to where they could quickly gather dry wood.

"What do you think, Feuille?" Loren asked.

It was already time to borrow the knowledge of the elves. After staring at the forest a bit and twitching his ears, Feuille turned to him.

"We should be fine here. I don't sense any dangerous animals nearby."

"I see, then we'll go with that."

Their plan settled, all that remained was to do it. Loren lowered the bag from his back, took out a large tent, and deftly set it up.

He dug a hole for a fire at a safe distance and surrounded it with stones he found nearby. Once that was done, he dug a somewhat deeper hole farther away, just into the forest and hidden by the thicket, hanging a lantern on a nearby branch just in case.

While Loren was doing all of this on his own, Lapis and Feuille gathered dry branches and piled them into the fire pit.

"That's about right for a one-night camp."

Once the lantern and firepit were lit, their rudimentary camp was complete.

They had kept their bags light, shirking any cooking supplies, so it wasn't like they could roast anything over the fire. But they could boil water and heat up their dried rations. This was plenty.

"If we're heading in tomorrow morning, we should tuck in early," Loren said.

"What about lookout duty?"

"You and me on rotation. Fifty-fifty."

"Umm, what about..." Feuille started.

"Just sleep. Sleeping well is part of a child's duties."

Feuille was determined to help out with the watch shifts, but Loren turned him down. In any case, Loren didn't think even an elf child would be much good on lookout duty. He would still have to take his shift alongside one of the adults, so it hardly spared them the work. Feuille was better off sleeping until morning. Regardless, Feuille seemed put out to think he wasn't needed, his expression glum.

"We'll be depending on your memory tomorrow," Loren told him. "Get some rest and preserve your stamina until then."

Loren ruffled the boy's head again and brought back his smile.

I see. When a child looks gloomy, it seems to make everything around him gloomy, Loren thought.

For some reason, Lapis decided to push her head against his arm.

"What?"

"Mr. Loren, please pet me like that."

"Consider your age."

"It feels like you're giving Mr. Feuille preferential treatment!"

He would lose nothing by ignoring her, but he didn't want to risk her bad mood. With little choice in the matter, he took a deep breath and placed a hand on her head. He petted her gently, just enough that she wouldn't think he was half-assing it.

Her eyelids lowered, closing almost completely. After reveling in the sensation for a long moment, she pulled her head out from under his hand and clenched her fist.

"Now, I can fight another day!"

"What's that supposed to mean?"

She wasn't making any sense, but she wasn't in a bad mood, so maybe he could take the win. However, his expression soon turned from tired to tense.

As he reached for his sword, Lapis's complacent aura transformed into one of grim anticipation. A beat after that, Feuille's long ears twitched.

"Huh? This is..."

"I knew we should have made the camp farther from the forest," Loren complained.

"That's just hindsight speaking," Lapis told him.

They spoke casually, but their ears were locked on the sound of footsteps approaching.

"There's a few of them. Do you know what they might be?"

Loren drew his heavy black blade from his back. Lapis took a stance to protect Feuille as the kid desperately racked his mind for the identity of the creatures stalking toward them.

"These sounds...probably forest wolves."

"Those things, eh."

Loren had heard the name before and even fought a few of them. They were wolves that lived in forests and hunted in packs. Additional fun fact—forest wolves were a leading cause of death for copper-rank adventurers who entered the woods for easy quests. Immediately after Feuille revealed their enemy, the wolves shot out of the forest in a cacophony of pants and growls.

Loren swung, managing to sever the one at the lead from snout to tail. On the return swing, he caught the ribcage of a wolf pouncing to bite him, splattering its organs over the ground.

"Oi, the hell is this?"

Loren had taken two out in the blink of an eye, but another had already launched itself at him. Without the time to ready his sword, he kicked it away. In that moment, he took in their situation and got an unhappy shock.

Forest wolves hunted in packs, so Loren had expected a good handful. However, the number of wolves that surrounded their camp profoundly exceeded expectations, even minus the three he'd taken care of.

"Maybe a few packs got together?" Lapis suggested.

Keeping Feuille close, she held out her right palm. A wolf tried to take this prime chance to tear an arm off, but instead found its head facing the wrong direction with a dull crack.

Paying no mind to their fallen comrades, another wolf launched, then another, each ending up with their heads twisted at odd angles, and each slumping lifeless to the ground.

"Eh? Ehhh?!"

Feuille watched, unable to believe the carnage wrought by the pretty priest guarding him. She waved her right hand, staring down at the forest wolves. They didn't seem eager to retreat.

Lapis cocked her head as she snapped the neck of another. "This is strange. Are pups like this always so determined?"

Each individual wolf wasn't so dangerous on its own, but they knew the strength of the pack and weren't cowards. Still, your average wolf was intelligent enough to run upon seeing its fellows so easily slaughtered. The wolves coming at them were sliced through and broken one after the next, yet they showed no sign of backing down.

"What's with them?"

"Who knows? Maybe they really want to put us on the menu?"

Lapis's right hand stabbed at the jaw of a forest wolf lunging at her throat. She smacked it to the ground and crushed its head underfoot; Feuille's face twitched.

"I don't want a child to see this, but what else can we do?"

"Get him into the tent!"

The sword Loren swung with only one hand turned several

wolves into lumps of flesh in midair. His left hand had a grasp on another's windpipe. It thrashed to escape his grip, but it was quickly crushed, bone and all. Its limbs went limp as the life left its body.

"Won't we be even more worried if he's out of sight?"

"That's... I get where you're coming from," Loren conceded. He dropped the corpse at his feet to grip his sword with both hands. "Ugh, I'd be happier if they were at least edible. What am I supposed to do with all of this?"

At some point, Lapis had given him a lecture about forest wolf meat being inedible to humans. Each time he swung his sword in a wide arc, even more bodies piled up, so much useless garbage.

"We might need to move camp anyways."

With so many bodies, the thick smell of blood filled the air. The ones Loren's blade tore through gave off the stench of viscera as well. Even if they managed to drive the wolves away, this was no place to sleep.

"Moving again? Do we have to?" Lapis sounded reluctant.

"Complain all you want, do you want to camp here?"

She couldn't refute that, or Loren didn't *think* she could. However, it seemed Lapis had an idea. She grabbed Feuille by the nape, shoved him in the tent, and shut it. Just as Loren was wondering what she was doing, he saw her lift her left hand.

"Hey, you're not going to..."

"Let it swirl before mine eyes, o crimson flames, ye storm and burst. *Firestorm!*"

Lapis spun her spell before Loren could get a word in edgewise. In no time at all, a powerful swirl of flame manifested. Not just one either. Four massive maelstroms of fire roared to life around the campsite, dragging wolves into the current of their blaze as the flame rose toward the heavens.

"Tee hee. Did you see that masterful magic? My spells have gone up in range and firepower, now that I don't have to constantly send mana to my left arm!"

She was so darn proud of herself. Loren silently clenched his fist and knocked it ungently on the crown of her head.

Lapis yelped, holding her head with both hands as she squatted down on the spot. Her control was cut, and the flaming whirlwinds burnt out, leaving not a trace behind.

"You didn't have to..." she whined.

"Now look here, how were you going to explain if someone saw that?!"

"A mysterious sage came to our rescue at a critical moment!"

"You want another one?" Loren shook his clenched fist.

Lapis turned a bit pale, shaking her head as she wrapped her palm around his knuckles. "Please don't, you'll leave a permanent dent."

"Good grief. Well, that should have sent them running..." A forest wolf interrupted Loren, leaping out of the trees toward his unprotected neck. Loren swung his right arm up and got teeth in it for his trouble.

"Mr. Loren?!"

"Bastard..."

Loren couldn't believe his eyes. Lapis's magic had turned most of their pack to ash, and yet the remaining wolves lingered, as if they had waited for the flames to dissipate before taking their chance. This one had jumped at Loren the second he let his guard down.

The forest wolf that was clamped onto him growled as it tried to sink its fangs deeper, but Lapis grabbed its upper and lower jaw between her slender fingers. In the next instant, she had pulled it off Loren as if its bite strength meant nothing. She kept right on pulling until she had torn it in two.

"Are you okay, Mr. Loren?!"

"It's nothing. But what the hell is up with them?"

These wolves paid no mind to the deaths of their brethren and didn't shy from the massive flames. It seemed they were dead set on chewing their enemies to bits, totally obstinate. Loren wondered if they had gone mad. Their survival instincts had gone right out the window.

"Do we really look that delicious?" he asked.

"Your meat looks pretty tough, Mr. Loren. I doubt they'd want you for dinner. It would have to be either me or Mr. Feuille."

Loren didn't know what to say to that. It wasn't like he wanted to be delicious, but it was a little demoralizing for her to say he was unappetizing to his face.

"My guts aren't gonna be as bitter as a demon's, though."

"Are you trying to say I'm full of vile blackness?!"

"Which means Feuille is tastiest, by process of elimination."

"I'm delicious too, aren't I?! I'm not going to lose to some brat! My skin is young and my flesh is supple, like a perfectly ripe peach!"

Had anyone else been there to hear her shouting, they would have arrived at some strange misunderstandings. Loren paid her no mind, instead counting the remaining wolves.

Their numbers weren't as impressive now. The ground had been burnt by Lapis's spell, but they stood there even as the heat scorched their paw pads. They were no closer to giving up.

"Looks like we have to kill every last one of them..."

Loren had never heard of an animal that kept fighting until its every ally was dead. It was, however, growing increasingly easy to imagine this pack of forest wolves would come for them until the last of them was put down. A chill ran down Loren's spine.

This was not natural, not by any means.

"Don't let it get to you, or they'll take you by surprise again," Lapis warned him, her voice colder than before. "Though I won't stop you, if you want to be their meal."

"This is no joke."

Burnt and broiled by the hot ground, one of the wolves ran out of strength and fell before it could pounce. The others could clearly see the danger that felled it, but that didn't stop them from taking the very same path.

Loren gripped his sword, already sick of the smell of burnt hair, skin, and flesh. But he couldn't help feeling an iota of hesitation.

"We can think about the cause later," Lapis told him. "For now, we have to cut through."

"I know. I get that, but..."

Two forest wolves came at him. With a flash of his sword, he tore through their bodies like paper. One died immediately from its injuries, but the other wasn't so lucky. Its innards spilled from the gaping hole in its belly, but still it dragged its failing body to Loren's leg and snapped at Loren's ankle. It didn't stop until Loren crushed its skull.

"This is creeping me out."

"Yes, this is not...quite normal."

Ultimately, the forest wolves didn't stop until the last one was a corpse. Not a single wolf attempted to flee.

The next morning, they cleared up their campsite and finally set foot in the Black Forest. Loren had spent a chunk of the night gathering the remains of the forest wolves and piling them up for Lapis to incinerate.

He cleaned up the scattered blood and guts as best he could, gathering them up into cloths and tossing the bundles into the fire, but the metallic smell of blood and the sour stench of organs continued to linger. No one slept very well that night.

Neither Loren nor Lapis was happy about staying put, but after fighting off the wolves, they had lost the willpower to pick everything up and reassemble it elsewhere. One shared look was enough to communicate that they were both ready to put up with the stench, and so they stayed there for the night.

"Are you all right? Both of you?" Feuille asked, looking understandably worried.

The two adults had kept watch on rotation, but even while it was their turn to sleep, the foul odors had prevented them from resting properly. Not that one sleepless night was enough to slow them down, but the sleep deprivation showed on their faces.

Incidentally, after Lapis had shoved him in the tent, Feuille had crawled into his sleeping bag to anxiously wait out the attack. He had fallen asleep like that and only woke once the sun rose.

"It's all right," Loren told him.

"I'd like to borrow a bed once we reach that settlement of yours," Lapis said sullenly. A sleepless night hadn't drained her strength any, but it sure had made her grumpy.

Feuille hurried to nod. "Please, take it easy. I'm sure everyone will welcome you."

"I hope so. Guess I'll be counting on that."

Honestly, Loren wanted to turn around and head straight back. The previous night's attack had been altogether too creepy. He didn't mind being attacked. Hell, he expected it when they set up camp near any forest animal's territory. However, those wolves had completely ignored the inborn survival instincts they should have cleaved to. That was proof that something strange was afoot within the forest. Adding that to the disappearance of the elves from town and the missing people who had gone to investigate, the Black Forest was growing more and more ominous.

Loren proceeded with caution.

"How long will it be until we reach your settlement?" Lapis asked, following along behind him.

Feuille looked around, thought a bit, then answered, "We should be there if we walk around a stound."

"That's quite far."

Elves were at ease in the forest. They moved efficiently, in ways humans couldn't grasp, and their common sense told them which paths were the safest to follow. When dragging a human down those paths, the same didn't hold true. An elf could easily clear stretches where a human would trip up or stumble through the undergrowth.

"So you shouldn't take his estimate at face value," Lapis whispered to Loren.

He didn't nod back. Instead, he swiftly swept his hand through the air.

Lapis readied herself, not sure what was happening. Right before Feuille's startled eyes, Loren grabbed something in midair. He held it up to reveal a snake he had caught by the neck. It coiled around his arm, its body reaching from wrist to elbow; it had likely dropped from the trees above in a bid to bite one of their party. However, it was clearly not large enough to eat any of them.

Yet the snake still opened and closed its mouth, doing anything in its power to bite Loren's hand.

"Lapis, this reeks of trouble. Watch out."

With that warning, Loren crushed the snake until it went limp and lifeless. He carelessly tossed it into the undergrowth.

As the snake thumped into the bracken, there was frantic movement through the leaves, then violent tearing sounds and intense crunching. Feuille paled.

"What hellscape have we stumbled into?" Lapis asked as they listened to something devour the discarded snake. They picked up the pace, not eager to figure out what exactly the scavenger was.

"I'm surprised you elves can live in this danger zone," said Loren.

"It's not usually like that..."

At their feet, a scurrying mouse scooped up an insect and began chowing down on it. The mouse was suddenly stabbed to death by a strange vine striking from overhead, and the vine voraciously sucked out its body fluids. Insects flocked to the mouse's desiccated corpse, dismantling its dry remains. Then these insects became the meal of another mouse.

More crunching sounds made them look up to see the corpse of some animal impaled on a sharp branch, being feasted upon by a monkey-like beast.

I remember some birds eat like that, Loren thought, at which point a massive bird struck the monkey from behind. The bird grabbed its prize in its talons and took off to greater heights.

"Hey, what sort of place have we wandered into?" Loren wondered aloud. "Is this forest supposed to be so brutal?"

A new monkey replaced the one that had been taken by the bird, and this one swooped down on Loren from above. Loren whacked it away without looking. He dented its face with its fist, and it crashed into trees as it flew a good distance. Once it hit the ground, who knew what started going to town on its flesh. Its shrill shrieks and the rustling cause Feuille to jerk.

"What was that?"

"A forest ape, I think. But this is strange. They're omnivorous, but they usually live on fruit. They rarely attack other animals like that..."

"I don't really get it. I guess some days, you just want to have meat."

Loren knew that was nonsense even as he said it. But if he didn't make light of the situation, there was no way they could press on.

"Lapis, have you figured anything out? Any leads?" he asked, hoping to rely on the power of a priest to the god of knowledge.

Lapis made a bewildered face, staring in the direction he'd sent the forest ape flying.

Is she seeing something we can't? he wondered.

However, she shook her head and muttered, "I thought they were under the influence of something malevolent, but that doesn't seem to be the case. They're acting too aimlessly for some-one to be controlling them."

She'd barely gotten her last word out before something coiled around Feuille's torso.

He didn't have time to scream before his body was wrapped tight and yanked upward. Loren immediately grabbed the kid with his left hand, using his right hand to tear through the bind-ings—and something cried out in the trees.

That something was a massive frog over three feet tall, hanging upside down from the branches. It had tried to catch Feuille with its tongue.

Sure, it was a damn big frog, but it wasn't large enough to gulp down an entire ten-year-old. Loren delivered a kick to rock the tree, then stomped on the frog where it fell.

"This is a mess."

Insects immediately flocked to the dead frog. It was taken

apart before Loren's very eyes, and his stomach churned as he watched it practically melt away. Removing the bits of tongue still clinging to a stupefied Feuille, Loren patted him on the back.

"Fweh?!" Feuille sputtered.

"They'll just keep on coming if we stand around. I don't know what's going on, but there'll be trouble if we don't get to your settlement fast."

"G-got it."

The realization was a bit delayed, but Feuille finally noticed he had almost been eaten. His body quivered, but he understood something else would be after him if he loitered. He nodded and walked farther into the trees.

"Mr. Loren, I feel it's dangerous to press on like this without any preparations," Lapis said, her tone urgent. They trudged through the undergrowth, following where Feuille led them. "If the bugs start attacking us, my blessings and your sword won't be enough to fend them off in these numbers."

No matter how masterfully Loren wielded his sword, there was little he could do if he was attacked by a swarm of bugs. As things stood, they'd been blessedly sting-free, but it wouldn't be strange if the insects recognized them as food at any point in the next few moments.

"Then what are you suggesting?" he asked.

"Please borrow Ms. Scena's strength."

At this, Scena popped up. <*Me?*>

Of course, neither Lapis nor Feuille could see her, but Lapis went on regardless.

"I think we should deploy a faint energy drain and use it as a shield. That should be enough to take out the smaller bugs and animals without much life force, and it will simultaneously repulse the larger ones."

"The bugs aren't gonna turn zombie on us, are they?"

"You'll need to ask Ms. Scena to be careful. I don't know if she can do it or not."

He asked Scena if she could do what Lapis was proposing. The girl thought a bit, then thumped her chest.

<I'll try. Leave it to me, Mister.>

The moment Scena accepted the task, the foliage in front of them turned from green to brown. Caught by unlucky coincidence, bugs began dropping like, well, like flies. The small animals that crept up to eat these insects keeled over and went still.

< Thin, gentle, and vast. That's how I'm deploying my power.>

"We could market this as a bug repellent for the summertime."

As the undergrowth cleared and it became easier to see what lay beneath, they found the ground blanketed in insects and small animals. Any animals over a certain size would flee, at last fearful of their own death as all the surrounding life force was sucked away. The larger trees, which presumably had more strength than all the bugs and little plants, were not visibly changed.

"It's gotten quite a bit easier to walk."

With the plants withering away, there was nothing blocking their feet. The trees were still a hindrance, but they weren't so closely packed that it was difficult to squeeze between them. The party was suddenly moving at a much faster clip.

"Huh? Eh? What's going on?" Feuille remarked at this sudden change to the forest. He turned to Loren and Lapis, hoping they could explain why the plants were all shrinking and dyeing away for no reason, but it wasn't like they could be upfront about it.

Lapis looked away, while Loren let out a troubled laugh.

"It's a secret. Adventurers always keep an ace up their sleeve. Remember that."

Though Loren hoped no other adventurer had an ace like his. Feuille looked doubtful, but they urged him onward.

Feuille had explained that it would take a stound to reach the settlement on foot, but it looked like he had been measuring in elvish terms after all. It took nearly twice that time for them to see anything remotely resembling civilization.

It was by no means an easy journey. Every few steps, they came across one animal fighting another and the loser being devoured. They encountered the same kind of gory scene over and over. Poor Feuille, who had started out a bit pale, was white as a sheet by the end of it. Loren and Lapis were both thoroughly sick of the pattern.

"An incessant stream of attacks from animals and whatnot," Loren muttered. "Who knows what would have happened if we didn't have Scena?"

If Scena hadn't cast energy drain, they would have tussled with far more would-be predators. If the bugs set their sights on blood, neither Loren nor Lapis had any countermeasures. Perhaps they would been forced to retreat then and there.

With poor enough luck, they might have run out of strength more or less instantly.

<I still have plenty left in me. Leave it to me, Mister.>

Loren offered the girl his sincerest gratitude.

Soon, beyond a thicket, there was a fairly wide gap in the trees. It was surrounded by a fence that stood about human height. Beyond that, Loren could make out a few buildings made of rounded logs. The trees clustered thick around the buildings dimmed the entire area, but the sky was clear over the opening in the canopy, and it showered the clearing in vibrant sunlight.

"So that's your settlement?" Loren asked Feuille.

"That's right! This is..."

"I see. Glad you—"

Loren cut himself off. Feuille sounded cheerful enough, and the boy looked up at Loren as he stopped and peered through the shadow of the trees.

Loren didn't have time to pay Feuille any mind. He stared at the settlement, and Lapis came to stand beside him and stare as well.

"How is it?" he whispered to her.

"That question is so vague, I am unable to identify the answer," she replied, nonchalant. He sent her a grim look. Upon noticing that, she shrugged and added, "What are you asking about?"

"The settlement. How does it look to you?"

"Too quiet, and not a soul in sight."

Hearing this, Feuille peered at the settlement he had once called home. There were usually adults in armor at the entrance built into the fence. On a normal day, there would be more adults patrolling the perimeter, as well as elves of all ages going about their day behind it.

But now there wasn't a soul in sight. Perhaps something had happened to the settlement. Feuille grew anxious and felt the urge to rush in as fast as he could. However, Loren and Lapis continued to observe, and they didn't seem to want to get any closer.

"Umm..." said Feuille.

"I know what you want to say," said Loren. "Trust me, I do."

How long are we going to hide? When are we going in? That was surely what the kid wanted to ask. Loren scratched his head. He didn't want to go at all.

Feuille picked up on Loren's hesitation, and his big eyes grew bigger.

"Something's clearly up, right?" said Loren. "The sun's high in the sky, but I don't see anyone about. Something happened—it's practically screaming as much."

"My thoughts exac—Mr. Loren! Up!" Lapis warned him.

Loren immediately reacted, starting to swing the sword he'd kept drawn, but the instant he could clearly see his assailant, he let go of the blade with his left hand and used it to cover his face. His attacker coiled its long limbs around him and bit hard into his exposed hand.

"You gotta be kidding me," Loren muttered.

It had attacked him soundlessly from above—he hadn't even realized it was there until Lapis had warned him. Once he got a better look at it, he could tell it was a male elf with disheveled hair. The elf's canines were bared, and he was still young enough to be called a boy.

The elf boy panted harshly, growling like a beast as he ground his teeth with all his strength, attempting to tear away the flesh of Loren's arm. But the teeth of a child, no matter how harshly applied, could only leave deep marks in Loren's skin. It was impossible for him to really get at the meat, as it were.

His teeth nevertheless pierced Loren's skin and drew blood.

"Do elves eat people?" Loren asked.

He couldn't smack the elf away or crush him like he had the forest wolves—not in front of Feuille. For the time being, Loren stabbed his sword into the ground and attempted to peel the elf boy off his body. However, while Loren should have possessed the absolute advantage in physical might, the boy was surprisingly powerful. Try as he might, Loren couldn't tear him away, and they got stuck in an awful tussle, with each side unable to claim victory.

"Good grief. What do you think you're doing to Mr. Loren?" Unable to remain a bystander, Lapis reached out. She grabbed the boy's tattered clothes by the collar and pulled. She yanked hard in hopes of removing him, but the clothes ripped, and the boy's grasp on Loren remained strong.

Staring sullenly at the frayed cloth, Lapis lunged and grabbed the elf boy by the neck, forcefully tearing him away. To prevent the boy from biting Loren a second time—or going after her—she used her hold on his neck to chuck him straight at the settlement.

The boy flew with a considerable amount of momentum, drawing a parabola into the air. Even after he had landed, he rolled a while, tumbling with all Lapis's fury driving his trajectory.

"How is your wound, Mr. Loren?" Lapis asked.

"Not serious, but..."

His skin had been pressed down in the shape of the boy's teeth, and a few points were oozing blood. It wasn't much of a wound, but tackling and gnawing on strangers didn't seem like a typical pastime for elven children. It was as uncanny as the rest of what was happening in the forest.

What if something terrible entered Loren's body through this open wound and the boy's spit? He feared he would lose himself as the boy had. But soon, the bleeding stopped and the teeth marks slowly faded.

<Leave it to me. I'll manage!>

"How reliable..."

"Do you feel anything changing?" asked Lapis.

She looked concerned, and Loren took a silent moment to feel out his body. He shook his head. Perhaps the change, if there was one, wasn't immediate. He couldn't be relieved just yet. However, Scena declared that it would be all right, and he decided to trust her.

"I'm fine. The problem is over there."

The boy's tumble had only been stopped by his collision with the settlement fence. Loren didn't usually have a lot of mercy to spare for people who bit him, but he didn't feel like cutting an elven child down in front of Feuille, who still hadn't grasped the reality of the situation.

As Loren drew his sword from the ground and walked toward the settlement he'd been hoping to avoid, he made his way to the fence with the faint hope that Lapis's throw had knocked some sense into the kid.

He looked down at the elf boy, who convulsed in the dirt.

"Be careful, Mr. Loren."

"He's not getting up soon, not after that throw."

In his experience, a human would have needed a lot of time to recover from a landing like that. Elves were slimmer and more delicate than humans, with lower physical defenses. Lapis might well have injured the elf child so badly that he wouldn't be getting up again.

"Hey, you feeling any saner?" Loren asked, but all he got back were low, garbled groans. He was beginning to suspect that it was hopeless when the moans suddenly jumped in volume.

He readied himself and stepped back, only for the groans to gradually shift into screams. The boy's body writhed on the ground, twitching and convulsing as the elf tore at his own chest.

"What's going on?" Loren asked.

"Could he be diseased?" Lapis observed from behind Loren.

Feuille cried out and tried to approach the writhing boy, but Loren grabbed him by the scruff of the neck and hauled him back before he could get close.

"Sarion!" Feuille called, desperation in his voice. "It's me! Feuille! Don't you remember me?!"

There was a flash of rationality in the writhing boy's eyes.

Just maybe, Loren thought.

But then the boy named Sarion let out a muddled scream the likes of which they hadn't heard before. He coughed up a great gout of blood.

On closer inspection, the clothes he wore were, in places, soaked with blood, which was gradually dying them red.

"Is he injured?"

Lapis pointed at a portion of the boy's bloody clothes. "I don't think it's that simple."

Loren focused on that spot until he noticed something squirming under the cloth. Each time it moved, the boy's screams grew louder and more intense. Disturbed at the unfamiliar sight, Loren backed up, dragging Feuille with him.

"Sarion! Get a grip, Sarion!"

Sarion reached out as Feuille cried his name. Did he know Feuille was well out of arm's reach? Desperate, Sarion groped for help before suddenly falling still. Like a marionette whose strings had been severed, his hand fell to the ground, and he was silent.

"What made him like this?"

Loren left a dazed Feuille with Lapis and approached the corpse. The boy himself was dead, but the small lump was still wriggling and shifting under his clothing. Revolted as he was, Loren needed to see what it was lest they face the same fate. Loren steeled his resolve and flipped up the cloth.

"Whoa?!" He was unable to stifle the cry.

A small humanoid figure with wings on its back was digging into the boy's skin with nails and teeth, tearing into his flesh.

5 Predation to Investigation

AT FIRST GLANCE, the thing looked similar to Scena: a palm-sized girl with flaxen shoulder-length hair, a fluttering white dress, and two transparent wings sprouting from her back.

The key difference was the blood covering her from head to toe, which was made all the more uncanny by her cutesy features.

"The hell is this?" Loren murmured as the girl lifted her face.

The girl, who had been biting into the dead elf boy's body, stared at him. He almost gave in to the urge to force a smile, but that was smothered when she opened her bloodstained maw and leapt at him.

Inadvertently, truly inadvertently, Loren hauled back and smacked the little thing out of the air with his hand. A creature only the size of his palm couldn't possibly withstand his strength, meant for swinging that large sword around.

There was a small *thwap* and some meager resistance. That was the whole fight, and its grand conclusion: Loren's enemy smashed into the ground. She twitched and fell still, the grass and dirt around her splattered with blood.

"That's a fairy..." Feuille pointed at the girl, his voice quavering. "But why...they've never..." he trailed off in disbelief.

Not that Loren understood it either. Even so, they needed information. Loren was about to scoop up the fairy's body when he noticed the elf boy's corpse—the one she had been snacking on—convulse again.

"Don't tell me..."

As if waiting for this cue, patches of the boy's body began to swell. Loren, catching on quick, shouted at Feuille and at Lapis behind him.

"Get back! There are more of them!"

More palm-sized fairies ripped their way clear of flesh and clothing. Some looked like girls, others like boys; they had different hairstyles and facial features, but they all wore simple clothing; and all were stained red from head to toe in blood.

How had they entered that pitiful elf boy's body? The question remained, but first there was a more pressing issue for Loren to resolve. The fairies had evidently grown bored of the boy's taste, and they flapped their small wings to fly straight at the closest alternative—Loren.

Had they been normal monsters, he wouldn't have hesitated to swing the sword in his hands. Unfortunately, the countless fairies flying at him were too small for his massive blade. He could stir up some winds with his sword to fight off a few of them, but the swarm was larger than he could deal with.

Loren considered dropping his sword for some good old-fashioned unarmed combat, but it didn't seem like he could ready-up in time, and the more time he spent dithering, the less time he had to choose his means of survival. Before he knew it, those fairy faces with bloodshot eyes and gaping mouths were right in his face.

He resigned himself to suffering a few bites, throwing his arms up to bear the brunt and gritting his teeth. The pain he was expecting, however, never came. All he felt were several thuds against his defending arms.

Closing one's eyes was suicide on the battlefield. This had long been hammered into his head, and he kept them open the entire time. Past the wall of his arms, he could see something falling out of the air; when he looked down, he saw that the fairies attacking him had fallen like well-sprayed bugs.

<*Praise me, Mister.*>

Scena sounded cheery, and Loren could piece together what had happened. She must have realized that the fairies were too numerous to defend against through physical means, so she'd swiftly deployed the same energy drain she had used against the bugs. With their bodies being far smaller than humans, the life force these fairies possessed was similarly a good deal lower.

That being the case, no matter how many there were, Scena believed the drain would work against them. She had protected him from the fairies.

Sorry about that. You really saved me there. Loren hadn't

worried he would become fairy food like the elf boy, but he'd braced for some serious injury.

It had happened so suddenly; perhaps Scena had been acted on instinct, unable to restrain her power. The fairy bodies on the ground were almost completely dried out, desiccated husks like mummies. Loren picked up one of them to examine its wrinkled skin and wings.

"The fairy race isn't supposed to be so bloodthirsty... What happened?" Feuille asked.

"Who knows? All I can tell you is that they weren't, and now they are."

"Do you think that's why there's no one in my village—" Feuille stopped himself there, his imagination making him shudder as he looked at the empty houses. They'd caused quite a ruckus right on the settlement's doorstep, yet inside the walls, all was still.

"They don't seem to have been turned undead." Loren handed the fairy off to Lapis after giving it a good once-over.

It wasn't exactly normal to handle a dead body so casually, but Lapis didn't seem bothered as she took it. She stripped off its clothing to study it from all angles. "There are no traces of drugs, parasites, or magic. Apart from the drying out and the wrinkles, he looks perfectly normal."

"You didn't hesitate to strip him."

"He was a boy."

"That's not what I was asking."

Lapis, somewhat disgruntled by Loren's cold treatment, off-handedly tossed the fairy corpse over her shoulder. It flew through the air in a high arc to disappear behind the trees. The moment it hit the ground, they heard the sounds of animals squabbling over the new meal. Feuille turned pale.

"For now, I'll place a defensive blessing on Mr. Feuille." Lapis clapped her hands down on the boy's shoulders.

"You do that. I don't want to be suddenly bitten from the side."

"Are you...all right, Mr. Loren?" Lapis asked. "Well, I guess you have that sword, after all."

Loren gestured questioningly toward his sword with his free hand. He lifted it up, wondering what could be special about it.

Lapis stroked the blade and proudly stated, "This has a bonus function by which it protects the wielder. It holds back curses and other such malevolent things."

"Why do you know the functions of something we just happened to find in a weapon store?"

Truth be told, Lapis had procured it from who knew where to replace the last one Loren lost. Could she have arranged with the shop owner to have it sold to Loren specifically? Loren hadn't checked with her about his sword purchases, of course, and she hadn't said a word. But looking back on how strange the affair had been, Loren was sure of it.

"I am a priest of the god of knowledge, after all," she said.

"Quit raising the bar for that poor god's poor priests."

He was really starting to pity her fellow members of the cloth. There was no one around to hear besides him and Feuille, sure, but it would be a problem if Feuille began to hold strange expectations for Lapis's purported peers.

"Putting that aside, do you want to try entering the settlement? We need to investigate."

"Hell no, I don't *want* to. But you're right, we do need to investigate."

There could still be survivors. Even if there weren't, perhaps they would find some clues as to how this had happened. With sword in hand, Loren walked brazenly up to the front entrance.

Behind him followed Lapis, then Feuille, who she led by the hand.

What they saw once they crossed the boundary was far more terrible than Feuille could have imagined, though both Loren and Lapis had expected some version of it.

The village must have been attacked out of nowhere. Houses were broken into and completely ransacked. In one, there were signs that its residents had been preparing a meal; the table still held ruined remnants of food, but most had been messily gobbled up by someone or something.

They managed to find a few bodies as well. From the corpses alone, it was hard to say whether the elves had chosen to fight or run, but the bodies littered the sides of the paths and slouched against the building walls.

The bodies were as badly wrecked as the buildings. It was impossible to say what exactly had killed them.

"This doesn't look like an attack that fairies could have perpetrated," Lapis muttered as she inspected a body slouched against the rubble of a once-was house. "This building has been totally smashed in places. This must have been the work of a middling or large-sized monster or wild beast."

"Then it's pointless to search this forest for it."

There were too many likely candidates; they'd never be able to say for sure. Even if they did manage to pin the blame on some specific culprit, it would do little at this point. The settlement had fallen, and there were no survivors to be found.

"They tried to hide their children, I see." In a basement, they found a child's body in a large box. The parents had likely hidden the child there, praying they would survive until attack was over. However, their attackers had gotten to the child first. Their prayers had fallen on deaf ears.

"No, there was that one kid."

"Meaning he must have survived this long... Such a poor soul." Lapis folded her hands in front of her chest and murmured a short prayer.

It's almost like she's a priest or something, Loren thought for a moment. Then he remembered that she really was one.

"What...happened to everyone?" Feuille asked Loren. After taking in all the wanton destruction, his eyes were hollow. Loren could have given the kid a guess or two, but he didn't have a definitive answer. He glanced at Lapis.

"I think it's dirty to hand it off to me at a time like this," she said.

"I get that."

But he didn't have Lapis's way with words. He could try to tell Feuille his idea of what might have happened, but he didn't know if the boy would withstand the shock of Loren's delivery.

"Granted, what I'm thinking is probably a little different from what you have in mind, Mr. Loren." Lapis heaved a sigh, then turned to face Feuille's pleading eyes. "I don't know the exact population of your settlement, but there are too few bodies in evidence, given the scale of the village."

"That's..."

"Yes, it's possible that they were eaten, but this doesn't seem to have been an organized, calculated attack. I'd expect at least a few people to have been able to flee in the chaos."

A little light returned to Feuille's eyes. Loren nodded from the sidelines. When the settlement was attacked, those who couldn't fight would have run or hidden. In that case, it wouldn't be strange if they found villagers who had tried to get away. Loren couldn't say for sure that no one could have succeeded.

"We saw a rest town that was specifically, systematically wiped out before we met you. This seems different... And so, Mr. Feuille, do you have any idea where your people may have fled to?"

Perhaps someone had survived. Once that possibility was presented to him, Feuille steeled himself and offered up the sole refuge he could think of.

"The hidden village of the faeries?" Loren parroted.

Feuille looked up at him and nodded. The name was shady as could be, but Loren turned a blind eye to that and asked what sort of place this 'hidden village' might be.

"I'm sure you know that fairy-kind dwell in this forest. There is a village where the high-ranking among them live."

"Why would your people run there?"

Lapis had told Loren that elves and fairies were closely related. There was a bit of a size difference now, but they shared a common ancestor. Loren didn't know what had led to their split, but he did know that elves and fairies generally chose to establish their settlements in the same sorts of forested places.

"The fairies have a chieftain. We elves are closely linked to the fairies, and they offered to take us in during times of emergency."

"I see."

"Do you know the way there?" Lapis asked.

It was called a hidden village, so there probably wasn't an un-hidden road there. Unfortunately, Feuille just cocked his head, troubled. It seemed that, while he knew the circumstances, he didn't know the details.

Loren sighed and shrugged; there wasn't anyone else around to cough up an explanation. "Do we investigate the settlement again?" he asked.

"I think I've already had a good look at everything."

Though they were just confirming the situation, not expecting any answers, they had poked around a decent amount. The settlement wasn't very large, and Lapis didn't think she'd overlooked anything. However, perhaps their change in objectives would give her a fresh point of view, so she wasn't too strongly against a second round of investigations.

Hoping to raise their chances of finding something, Loren asked Feuille, "Is there anything you remember about the hidden village? It can be anything."

"U-umm..."

Feuille understood that his memory was the only thing they had to go on. He desperately racked his brain for any leads, but he wasn't able to recall anything relevant.

Time passed, moment by moment, as they stood twiddling their thumbs.

There was little to be gained without action. Loren called over to Lapis, "Let's leave Feuille to think about it. The settlement's still our best bet, since we don't have any other leads."

"You're right. We might find something worthwhile."

Loren couldn't help but feel anxious about Lapis's sticky fingers, but he forced himself to ignore it. Feuille was still mumbling and thinking, so Loren issued an order.

"Feuille, you wait here. We're going to check through everything again. Shout for us if anything happens. You got that?"

"O-okay."

Loren made sure to get a response before setting off with Lapis to reexamine the settlement. He hadn't been particularly fond of this investigation the first time around, and he grimaced as he once more searched through every nook and cranny. And who could blame him? The vivid remnants of the attack still dotted the entire settlement. Turning the houses upside down, having to inspect every element up close and personal, meant growing acquainted with the corpses and the blood. He took care not to think any unnecessary thoughts as he quietly set to work.

"Elves aren't usually the sort to decorate themselves with precious metals. They are the kind of people who would say,

'We're pretty enough as it is, why fix what isn't broken?'" said Lapis.

"That sounds really prejudiced... Wait, why are you talking about precious metals?" Loren demanded. "I'd love to hear it."

They were turning a shelf inside out, and he made his question rather threatening. Either Lapis didn't hear him, or she pretended she hadn't.

"They settle in the woods, and live off of hunting and gathering," she mumbled to herself, ignoring him. "They barely have any money... I'm not feeling too motivated."

"Oi, wait. What exactly are you looking for?"

"Why, information about this hidden fairy village. Am I not supposed to be?"

She answered as if it were entirely obvious—as if she didn't understand why he was asking. Loren knew something was off, but she hadn't given the wrong answer, so he returned to work.

"They conducted trade with human towns, so I'm sure the coins they pay them with must be somewhere... But where?"

"Wait, wait. What's that got to do with anything?"

Loren hurriedly placed a hand on her shoulder, turning her around to face him, However, once he had extracted her from her investigation, she glared up at him, thoroughly irked. "I'm conducting a proper search. You want a lead to the hidden village, right? What are you so worried about, Mr. Loren?"

She acted so confidently that, for a moment, Loren wondered if he'd misheard. The thought crossed his mind that Lapis was doing a proper job after all, and he released her shoulder.

He apologized to her as she straightened her clothes. However, before he could even get back to work, she said something that made him grab her again.

"Ah, I found a stack of silver coins." Lapis sounded exuberant as she pulled out a stack of coins rolled up in some kind of animal skin.

"Hey, hold it. It's been nothing but money and precious metals with you. You're not trying to use the confusion to play it off, are you?"

Lapis held up her new silver coins with an incredibly stern look on her face. "The dead have no use for money. Nor do they use the metals for decorative purposes."

"Sure, you have a point."

"Either this silver is left here to rot, or it fills the pockets of whoever happens to stop by. In that case, what's wrong with slipping it in mine?"

"I'm not gonna stop you from taking anything. But promise me you'll give it to the survivors if we find them."

Lapis was in the right only if the coins had no owner. In that case, Loren thought it was fine if the money left with her. However, they were searching for this fairy village precisely to find the residents of this one. The coins she held so tightly to her body belonged to those potential survivors.

"Mr. Loren, I'm suddenly losing the will to search on..."

There was no guarantee they would find the actual owners of the coins. However, if there were any survivors at all, they would have more right to the remains of the village than Lapis

PREDATION TO INVESTIGATION

header

did. Finding the fairy village meant searching for survivors, and finding survivors meant surrendering the money.

"Take this seriously, Lapis. We might not leave this place alive."

"Do you really think so?"

She sounded quite optimistic.

Loren didn't know whether to be relieved by the familiarity of her response or to scold her for her lack of situational awareness. Very possibly, a high-spec demon like Lapis didn't recognize something like this as a crisis at all. With the nagging feeling that neither of these options were quite right, Loren went back to work without a word.

Then she tapped him on the back.

"What's wrong?" he asked.

"Mr. Loren, I've forgotten one important thing."

Overpowered by her suddenly serious tone, he nodded.

She went on, "This village must have been attacked at least once, right?"

"Well, yeah. It was destroyed."

"Where do you think those attackers disappeared to?"

They hadn't stuck around, at the very least. Otherwise, their party wouldn't have been let in so easily, and they never would have been able to investigate this thoroughly.

"You're saying..."

Hopefully, the monster or wild beast or whatever had taken off for somewhere very far away.

"I don't know how many attacks it took for the settlement to fall... But I'm sure whatever it is, it remembers the good harvest it had here."

Loren understood the logic: if the creature had reaped a bounty before, instinct told it that it had a chance to reap well again. "That...might be true."

"Do you think it will come back?"

Lapis's nonchalant question cast a shadow over his heart. The animals in the forest had gone mad and were running amok. He wouldn't have been shocked if the whole lot had been reduced to their most basic instincts. Instincts like the same sort that led predators to return to their old hunting grounds.

It was altogether possible that what had attacked the settlement would imminently return.

"What's more, we entered without making any efforts to conceal ourselves."

"We're returning to Feuille." Loren moved before Lapis finished speaking. She followed him as if she knew full well what his response would be before he'd even started moving.

New prey had stepped into the hunting grounds. Once that information reached the hunter, there was only one thing left for it to do.

"Dammit! This place was dangerous as all hell!"

"We noticed a little late, didn't we?!"

They heard Feuille's scream in the distance.

Instead of conducting such a carefree investigation, they should have left the moment they confirmed the place had been destroyed. But they couldn't exactly change the past.

"Mr. Loren! The elf corpses!"

Turning to Lapis's voice, Loren saw little bodies tearing their way out of the dead. They were fairies, as far as he could tell. Loren clicked his tongue and picked up the pace. What hell was this happening?

"Fairies don't hatch from eggs, so they couldn't have been laid in advance—so why are fairies emerging from elves? Is it because they're closely related? But what prompted this transformation?"

Lapis continued muttering to herself as she watched the incomprehensible spectacle unfold.

But now was no time to pay mind to her. Protecting Feuille took priority, and Loren raced through the buildings until he found Feuille running toward them.

"Mr. Loren! The fairies are here..."

"I can see that! We're getting out of here, hold on!"

The dust rose as Loren hit the brakes. He grabbed Feuille's hand, pulled him up to tuck him under an arm, and shot off back in the direction he'd come from.

"Umm, oh... Already back, I see." Lapis was momentarily baffled by Loren's sudden shift. She turned her back to the massive legion of fairies that had been chasing Feuille, not looking particularly bothered by it. As the beating of wings grew louder and louder, she took off after Loren.

"I'm getting this vague feeling that we're in a dangerous situation. What shall we do?" Lapis asked as they raced through the forest. Loren didn't have the time to answer her.

It was already hard enough to run through the trees, and he had to be careful he didn't smack Feuille against anything. The kid was a lighter burden than carrying Lapis on his back, but the uneven ground fatigued him more quickly than orderly terrain, and his legs felt like they would lock up the moment he faltered.

"Can we do something with Ms. Scena's abilities?" Lapis asked.

<I'm trying already...>

Though of course, Scena's reply didn't reach Lapis. Only Loren could hear it.

Upon her apology, Loren glanced back—he could see fairies here and there dropping to the ground after suddenly losing strength, but the little creatures chasing them were either too spread out or too numerous or both. Scena's drain wasn't having much of an effect.

"If we stop, they'll swarm us and eat us to the bone! What do we do?"

"Do you want me to burn them?"

"You'd rather be incinerated than eaten?"

Lapis's magic was certainly powerful. She normally wouldn't have used her power freely while Feuille was watching, but given their predicament, this was no time to worry about witnesses. That being said, they were still running through a forest. If she used the magic she had wielded at the campsite, she would take the trees out along with the fairies. There was no telling how far that fire would spread.

Once that happened, they would be trapped, breathing in thick smoke.

"Can't you use anything that isn't fire?"

"Fire's my specialty... Everything else simply isn't flashy enough."

"Don't pick your magic based on looks!" Loren shouted, but he couldn't order her to pull new abilities out of thin air. "If we keep running like this, they'll catch up eventually."

"They're having a much easier time of the forest, given how small they are."

With his large build, Loren had to carefully choose the gaps he could shoulder through at a run, but the fairies could essentially slip through anything and come at him in nearly a straight line.

"Don't fairies ever get tired of flying?!"

"They're supposed to, but in that state, I don't think being tired is going to stop them."

Loren glanced back, taking note of the fairies' bloodshot eyes, bloodstained mouths, and clicking teeth as they flapped their wings in a frenzy. Their originally endearing faces made their fearsome expressions and eager chase so terrifying that Loren feared he would see this scene in his dreams. He quickly turned back to look ahead.

"And it doesn't look like they're willing to hear us out," he muttered.

"What shall we do?"

Lapis didn't sound too concerned, but her expression was starting to show stress. Loren decided not to bicker with her, instead shifting Feuille into a firmer grip and concentrating on running. If he swung his sword and charged at the fairy army, he would suffer heavy wounds in the process. Victory wasn't completely unimaginable, but he wasn't in the right mind to think up a plan to fight them all off or escape. Instead, all he could do was focus on running and hope Lapis would think of a good idea.

After a while Lapis addressed a question to Feuille.

"Do you know if there's a decently sized lake or marsh in the area?"

"There is. That way." Feuille pointed from Loren's arms. Confirming the direction, Lapis tapped Loren on the shoulder—quite a skillful maneuver while running—and spoke loud enough that the beating of wings couldn't drown her out.

"Let's head that way!"

"That way..."

"I don't know if it's a lake or what, but there's water! You should know what to do."

It didn't take much thought before Loren caught her meaning. Come to think of it, perhaps they *would* be able to escape the fairies like that.

"So we're treating them like they're bees?"

"That's right. Now, pray that the water is clean!"

There were numerous ways to escape when chased by stinging bees, and jumping into water was one of them. Most flying animals despised getting their wings wet and couldn't continue a chase underwater.

Loren didn't know what would happen if a fairy wet its wings, but Lapis seemed to think there was a high likelihood they would stop their pursuit. This would require a considerable depth of water, though—enough to submerge Loren from head to toe. If the water was clean, he could put up with getting a little wet. If it was green, muddy, or rotten, he would hesitate even if his life was at risk.

"Feuille! Is it a lake or a swamp?!"

"P-pardon?"

"If it's a swamp, tell me beforehand! I need to prepare myself!"

Loren was capable of diving into sewer water to save his own life, but he didn't want to do it without a moment to steel himself. He wanted to confirm it with Feuille, but his question had come so suddenly, and Feuille was being rocked around so violently, that no proper response was forthcoming.

While Loren demanded answers, the trees suddenly opened up and the water they were looking for came into sight.

"It looks like a lake, Mr. Loren!"

The water he could see was neither brown nor green. Rather, it looked utterly clear.

"No need to worry then! We're jumping in! Hold your breath!"

"Just like that?! No, give me a second! Ah, for—*Water Breathing*!"

Right before Loren leapt from the bank, Lapis cast what was either a spell or a blessing. He sank without knowing if it had worked.

The water was so clear that he could see quite a long way through it. Loren feared that if every animal in the Black Forest had gone insane, perhaps the water was tainted as well. Then even if they did escape the fairies, they would just be pursued by the aquatic life instead.

However, and while this was not unconditionally true, clear water was generally not suited for life. Furthermore, when it was this clear, surely he would see an attack coming. He wouldn't have to fear some ravenous fish getting the drop on him. As he peered up at the water's surface, he saw the tightly packed swarm waiting for them to rise again. A chill ran down his spine.

Bees were known to linger for a bit, but they gave up quickly enough. The fairies, however, seemed intent on waiting out their prey.

This ain't good, Loren thought, holding his breath. He had taken a great gulp of air before jumping, but that wouldn't last forever. Resurfacing would prove necessary once his lungs started to burn. But there were so many of those fairies up there, he wasn't quite sure he could get a safe breath.

That left him with the choice of suffocating...or popping his up out of desperation, just to have his face torn off.

Lapis interrupted these thoughts, tugging on his sleeve. He turned to her to see her mouth was open, her chest rising and falling as if she were breathing. Doing that should have caused her to cough up all the air in her lungs, but Lapis took another breath as if it was nothing, urging him to do the same.

<Mister, the spell she used made it possible to breathe underwater. *You're all right, please breathe normally.>*

Even watching Lapis, Loren couldn't quite believe it was possible, and he hesitated. It took this prompting from a Lifeless King, a master of magic, for him to gingerly open his mouth.

It was as if the water ran into some sort of wall along the way.

It couldn't enter his mouth at all. Instead, his throat was filled with cold air that settled in his chest.

He checked Feuille just to be sure, and found that the kid was also in the midst of confirming that he could breathe. They weren't going to drown for the time being, and Loren was momentarily relieved.

Lapis took him by the hand and pulled. Given their difference in physique, and the fact they were underwater, her tugging barely moved him, and for a moment he wondered what she wanted to do. However, it seemed she couldn't speak underwater, so Scena explained instead.

< *The magic won't last forever, Mister. You need to swim somewhere where you can resurface safely, or you'll die anyway.*>

Even though they had momentarily escaped their fate, they would still ultimately drown. That didn't sound promising at all. Loren swam after Lapis, searching for somewhere to hide from the fairies overhead.

However, no matter how far they went, those black shadows loomed just above the surface. The lake itself wasn't so large, and the fairies were absurdly numerous—enough to completely cover it.

He wondered what to do as he stared at the shadows of the swarm overhead. In fact, he grew a bit resigned, and returned his eyes to the water to see Lapis swatting something away. He tilted his head.

Was one of the fairies capable of coming down after them? He approached her and his eyes widened at the sight of a fairy underwater with them.

"Wai—please wait a second! Listen to what I'm saying!"

The fairy didn't try to leave even as Lapis continued swatting at it. It seemed to be a woman.

The fairy's voice was clearly audible underwater. At her words, Loren stopped moving and Lapis pulled back her hand. Seeing the two of them had heard her, the fairy swam circles around Lapis, pausing in front of her face.

"Human, human? Are you two still normal? Did you run away from them? If that's the case, I can help you out. We need some help too."

Every fairy they had met thus far had torn and bit at them without uttering a word. This one, however, seemed to be able to breathe underwater by some magic, and she could speak as well. Most importantly, she was open to a dialogue.

"For now, please follow me. I want you to hear us out."

Her chestnut hair swaying underwater, the fairy flapped the wings on her back as she took off deeper into the lake. There didn't seem to be any other way out, so Loren and Lapis followed obediently.

THE Strange Adventure OF A Broke MERCENARY

6 Agreeing to a Request

IT WAS A SHOCK to be so suddenly met by a fairy who had maintained her sanity. Following a "fairy's guidance" did have a cool ring to it, but it wasn't like they had many options. Cool or not, they quickly found themselves swimming after her.

The black shadow of the mad fairy swarm still loomed overhead. It was strange to swim while breathing normally, and nothing felt quite real to Loren as they were led to a cave at the bottom of the lake.

The mouth of the cave was just barely big enough for a human to squeeze through, and it became a vertical shaft just a short way down. This too could only fit one person at a time. While the tight fit was no issue for Lapis and Feuille, Loren was unable to make it through with his sword on his back. He needed Lapis to go up first. She pulled the sword up for him, and he climbed up alone.

He grabbed onto the ledge above to hoist his body out of the water. Loren dripped onto the stone and shook himself like a soaked dog. Looking around, the first thing he noticed was the soft white light that lit the area.

"Ick... I'm soaked."

He looked toward the voice to see Lapis plopped cross-legged on the ground, wringing out her priestly vestments. Loren and Feuille weren't dressed so heavily and so were a bit better off on a scale of soggy to drenched; however, even Lapis's simplified robes, suitable for the adventuring sort of priest, were made of a good bit of fabric. Once soaked, they looked terribly heavy and unpleasant.

"This is all because you instantly threw yourself in the lake, Mr. Loren."

"What else was I supposed to do?"

"I only had time to cast *Water Breathing*. I had other spells that would have prevented us all from getting wet—and protected us from the water pressure."

Lapis glowered at him resentfully, but Loren didn't think she'd had time to prepare so much magic. He didn't think that voicing this particular opinion would put her in a good mood or anything, so he maintained his silence.

"I'm just going to strip. I can't move like this."

"You serious?"

Lapis, it seemed, quickly came to terms with the fact that she couldn't blame Loren. Complaining mightily, she whacked and squeezed her robes however she could to make them even just a little more bearable to wear. Eventually, she gave up on this endeavor completely. The weight and rub of damp fabric on her skin was unbearable, and she scowled as she vigorously wriggled out of her clothes.

Loren couldn't help but wonder why she thought it was perfectly fine and dandy for her to strip without hesitation when a man was around. On the other hand, squelching around in those damp clothes definitely sounded unpleasant, and he couldn't force her to keep them on—especially not when he was fighting the urge to take his own clothes off and dry them by a fire for a while. Not that even knew whether there was anything burnable in this cave, or whether there was a safe place to start a fire.

These thoughts were cut off by something floating in front of his face.

"Can you talk?"

It was the fairy that had brought them here. Her dress wasn't wet, nor were her hair or wings. Perhaps she had deployed all that magic Lapis mentioned.

"Hey? Hey? Can you understand me? Human? Human?" the fairy said with slow, drawn out words.

"Yeah, I can hear you, and I can understand you."

One way or the other, this fairy was their savior. It seemed proper to treat her courteously. Once Loren replied to her, the fairy smiled and perched on his shoulder.

"As for introductions, I am Cornet, of fairy-kind. Nice to meet you."

"She doesn't sound very bright." Lapis offered her frank opinion of the fairy.

Loren tried glaring at Lapis, then immediately looked away.

She'd gone right on stripping since he last glanced at her, and now she'd discarded everything apart from her chemise and under-garments. She kneeled there, her clothing in a heap beside her.

In short, her midriff was completely exposed. Loren didn't intend to look, but the sight was burned into his mind.

"Huh? You're bright red, Mr. Loren."

"Shut it. Cover up a bit, will you?"

"I don't see why I would... You're the only one looking, Mr. Loren."

"That's the problem," Loren said curtly, hiding his red face.

After staring a while at him, looking as if she didn't understand in the slightest, Lapis grinned. "What's this I hear? Is it possible that you're embarrassed?"

"Lapis, I don't know how to break it to you, but it's hard for me to like a girl with no sense of shame."

Loren needed to hammer this point home before she could get comfortable teasing him.

Lapis frantically collected her garments and attempted to cover her self. However, she wasn't feeling too inclined to pull the damp swathes of fabric back over her head. She brought the bundle close to her chest, the pulled it away, then tucked it back against her for a bit. Finally, she looked at Loren, troubled.

"Err, Cornet, was it?" Loren sighed. "We're drenched, as you can see. Do you know any way we can dry our clothes?"

"If that's what you want, please follow me. Our home is thataway."

The fairy girl—Cornet—took off from Loren's shoulder with a gentle flutter, beckoning as she slowly flew deeper into the cave.

Loren called out to Lapis (and Feuille, who had been sitting sodden on the floor), and together they gave chase.

"What's going on with this place?" Lapis asked, clutching her drenched clothes in front of her as a temporary measure. "It's some manner of cave, as far as I can tell."

Cornet tilted her head, not seeming to understand what Lapis was asking. "That's right. We're underneath that place you guys call the Black Forest."

"Then how is it so bright down here?"

"Well, that's because glowmoss grows on the rocks, you see. I don't know what makes the moss glow, though."

At this explanation, Loren peered closely at the nearest stone wall. As Cornet said, there a thin coating of moss, and somehow that moss was glowing bright enough to illuminate the entire cave.

"This is the sort of moss you often see in natural dungeons and the like. It's not as rare as you might think," Lapis explained in response to his dubious look.

"Is this different from those walls we saw in the ruins of the ancient kingdom?"

"Just because they both glow doesn't make them the same thing, Mr. Loren."

In a ruin of the ancient kingdom—which had turned out to be a nefarious goblin breeding facility—the walls had let off light due to their base materials. However, Lapis denied that they were in any way similar.

"From scarcity to luminosity to price point, every part of them entirely differs."

"Hey, people, you can look at the walls later. Please follow along. You'll catch a cold like that," Cornet said, concerned for her dripping guests. For now, they put off inspecting their surroundings and hurried after her.

Some way from the water, the cave-like corridor opened up into a dome-shaped plaza. The ground here was lined with small stone buildings, each rising only to Loren's waist. He could have taken it for a miniature model if not for the small winged figures passing from building to building. It was clearly much more than some replica.

"The big people are here!"

"They're here!"

When Cornet called out, fairies, both boys and girls, floated up from all around and flew around them in wide swoops. Loren readied himself, fearing an attack, but Lapis stopped his hand before he could reach for his sword.

"It's all right. I don't sense any hostility."

"Y-yeah... Sorry. Couldn't help myself."

"I understand the feeling."

Lapis clearly hadn't forgotten how it felt to be hunted by fairy-kind. She had witnessed just as many terrors wrought by the little ones as Loren had and found his defensive stance quite understandable.

"Everyone dry your clothes in here, okay?"

Cornet pointed them to a tunnel in a sidewall. On approaching it, Loren saw that it was too narrow for any human to pass through, but it led somewhere even farther into the cave system. A breeze, comfortably warm, whistled up through the gap.

"I was wondering why it didn't feel cold down here. So this is what you use to regulate the temperature."

"You can put your clothes near the entrance. The warm wind should help."

"Let's take her up on that, Mr. Loren. Our clothes should dry decently fast if we place them here where it's warmest."

"So, so, while your clothes dry, I want you to listen to my story." Cornet's expression clouded over ever so slightly as she floated up to Loren again.

"Right, come to think of it, you said you needed help," Loren said, watching Lapis spread her clothes out near tunnel entrance, positioning them to catch the breeze. "Try us. We've got to repay you for saving our skins. We'll hear you out, even if it's a bit crazy."

Once her own clothes had been laid out, Lapis began urging Feuille to strip down. The boy was more than a little flustered.

Cornet, with a serious look on her face, circled around Loren until she was looking him straight in the eye. She clenched her fist, telling him in that same steady, drawn-out voice, "I want you to kill the fairy chieftain."

"Is this a power struggle or something?" Loren asked. That was, after all, the reason most people wanted to assassinate their superiors. But something about Cornet made him doubt that was the case here.

Loren didn't know what sort of people fairies tended to be, but they didn't seem the sort to engage in the ambitious infighting that humanity spent so much time and effort on. It was something about the way the fairies spoke, the air they exuded. In fact, when

Loren brought up a coup, Cornet didn't seem to understand what he was going on about.

Loren apologized, urging her to go on.

"As I said, I want you to hunt down our chieftain."

"That's quite a thing to ask someone to do for you. What happened?"

"Well, the chief, you see. He went funny in the head."

Behind him, Lapis realized Feuille wasn't going to take his soaked clothes off. The boy put up a desperate resistance as she grabbed at his shirt, but Loren ignored their tussling. Cornet took a seat in a cavity of the bare rock face, crestfallen, her shoulders drooping.

According to her, for some time now, little by little, the fairy chieftain had been acting stranger and stranger. Fairies were whimsical, mischievous, and curious by nature. They often played pranks on the elves who lived in the forest and the humans who visited. It had all started when the king's pranks went beyond the realm of good clean fun.

"They really were just silly little things until then. Trust me."

"Give me a few examples, for reference."

"For instance, switching the salt and sugar the elves used, and splashing muddy water over the humans walking in the forest. That was about it."

"That's plenty troublesome... Whatever, go on."

"We continued arranging our cute little japes, but one day, the chief commanded us to raid the food storage of an elf settlement."

Without food, the elves would starve. Sure, they could seek help from other settlements, and perhaps they wouldn't die, per se, but the damage would be considerable. Though the forest was abundant in its blessings, the elves would need to put in back-breaking work to compensate for such a loss. Some fairies had rebelled, standing up to the king to say such an act was no longer in the realm of a joke.

The fairy chieftain had forced them into it anyway. They had stolen every last scrap and crumb of food from the settlement they chose.

"We begged the chief to return the elves' food—we did. He didn't listen, and he ate all the stolen food himself."

"All of it?! That's incredible. It must have been a lot."

"But it didn't end there! Encouraged by his success, the chieftain and the fairies around him began raiding other elf settlements as well."

"The elves must've been furious."

Loren glanced at Feuille to see Lapis had successfully wrestled him down to his underwear. Lapis hummed as she spread the kid's clothes out to dry, but for some reason, the boy kept his arms clutched over his chest, face bright red. When he noticed Loren's attention, Feuille shook his head.

Apparently, Feuille didn't know anything about these raids. Loren turned back to Cornet.

"Oh, they were! Livid, I tell you!" Though her tone was still the same, sorrow wormed its way into her words. Loren thought she was genuinely sorry for angering the elves, but the truth was far worse. "The elves came to protest. Me and everyone else, we were sure the chief would apologize."

They "were sure"—which meant that wasn't how it had gone down. Not that an apology would have been enough to make up for their crimes. But if the elves would have been happy with it, Loren didn't see any other solution that wouldn't fan the flames. Without an apology, no one could move forward with peaceful coexistence in the Black Forest.

Cornet pulled her chin in, lowering her eyes. "Funny story. The chieftain murdered every elf who came to him."

"Real funny," Loren retorted.

This king had greedily snatched the elves' food, devoured it, then killed the victims who had already suffered at his hand. Had this happened in the human world, no doubt it would have incited a war.

Unfortunately for the elves, they acted as independent settlements rather than as an entire race, or even an entire kingdom. Worse, if it came down to a magical fight, the fairies outpaced elves in mana capacity and technique. On top of that, they had been up against the chieftain, strongest among the fairy-folk.

"Don't get me wrong. The fairies faced considerable losses too, you know."

This had been a tragedy for Cornet's people, but she had hoped it would finally bring an end to the chief's rampage. If the dent in his fighting force was large enough, the chief's personal strength didn't matter. Without an army at his back, he couldn't hope to enforce his terrible demands.

Yet the chief had resorted to inconceivable means to replenish his losses and set his sights on still other elf settlements.

"So they started eating elves?" Lapis piped up.

Feuille's face stiffened at this, and Cornet hung her head.

"What's that mean?" Loren seemed to be the only one left in the dark. He posed the question to Lapis, as she seemed most knowledgeable.

"Elves are closely related to faeries," she explained. "But fairies are just a tad higher ranking. They're made of the same base materials, so it would be possible for a fairy to use their power to interfere with an elf's body. If done right, they could theoretically produce more fairies from elves. Not that this is common practice or anything."

She spelled out the terrible details as if this was all very normal, her disclaimer an offhand acknowledgment.

"This does explain the elves eaten from within and the fairies emerging from their corpses," Lapis continued. "In summary, this chieftain of yours has spread out his power, placing a large portion of the Black Forest under his influence."

"Exactly right," Cornet acknowledged.

Which made the fairy chieftain the cause of the forest's aberration. The situation wouldn't end unless that cause was removed.

"We can't leave the chief to his own devices. The fairies of the forest will be persecuted, and the elves will be hunted to extinction."

"That's why you want us to kill him?" Loren asked.

"Of course, I don't want our chieftain to die."

But Cornet couldn't see any other way. A chief who didn't listen to the words of his fellow fairies would hardly hear out the objections of a human. After killing all those elves, it was hard to imagine the chief taking humans into consideration at all. The party would probably have to fight him the moment they met.

"But hold up. What made the chieftain go mad? He wasn't always like that, was he?"

"True, true... But I don't know anything about that."

"Do you have any ideas? Perhaps he ate something he shouldn't have, or wore something he usually didn't?" Lapis asked.

Cornet thought for a while, her brow creased. Meanwhile, Lapis stealthily reached out to undo Loren's own drenched clothes. He smacked her hand away and only took off his coat to give to her.

"Umm, well, there is... But I don't know if this is the cause."

"Anything you can offer. It's always better to have more information."

Cornet nodded. "The truth is, we fairies happen to love shiny and pretty things."

The first thing that came to Loren's mind was glass. For some reason, certain birds would spend their time gathering sparkly objects, and their nests would be filled with glass shards. They would pick up anything that caught their eye; occasionally, they would find silver or gold coins and precious gemstones. It seemed the fairies shared a similar predilection.

"Everything we collect is gathered at the chief's place and

distributed from there. We use that stuff to decorate the village. I just remembered one of the kids brought in something strange a while ago."

Don't pick it up if it's so strange, thought Loren. But his stern logic meant nothing to fairies. Cornet stood atop the rock she'd perched on and spread her arms out.

"It was around this size," she told Loren. "A shiny, glowing metal box. There were symbols I'd never seen before carved on the surface."

"Hold on a second."

Her arm span was about the same as her height. Meaning whatever the fairies had picked up, it was about human-palm-sized. In that case, Loren had seen a box very similar to the one described in a place he'd been recently.

"Hey, Lapis. I remember seeing a box like that just the other day..."

"What a coincidence, Mr. Loren. I was thinking the same thing."

On their previous quest, in a practical exam conducted at an adventurer training academy, they came across one of the relics of an adventurer named Wolfe. Within that relic an entity had been sealed, one known as the dark god of sloth. It had been a metal box with complex symbols inscribed over the surface, just like the one Cornet described.

"Am I the only one hoping this *is* a coincidence?" he asked.

"I wish it were," said Lapis. "But I'm not coming up with any other ideas."

If it really was what they were imagining... Loren's mood took a heavy hit. Last time, their opponent had run away on his own. Perhaps he had been feeling lazy because he had only just revived. Or perhaps because he was, after all, the god of sloth, he just hadn't been particularly motivated. His awakening had not gone without casualty, but the damage had been thankfully relatively contained for someone called an dark god.

While there was no telling what sort of god was in this new box, the changes in the fairy chieftain made its effects abundantly clear. This dark god was probably less prone to running off for a nap.

"It's not like we can pretend we don't know anything."

"Mr. Loren, that kindness will be the end of you, one of these days."

The least troublesome option would be to find a way back aboveground—to pretend they never saw anything and put the Black Forest behind them. Loren knew that, but having heard the gory details, he couldn't just wave goodbye and leave the fairies to it.

"Cornet saved us, and we've got a debt to repay. Now that we've heard the story, we could at least put our heads together and see if there's anything we can do about the chief."

"It seems 'mind our own business' isn't an option for you. There really is no saving you, Mr. Loren. Ms....ah, Cornet, was it? Please answer my questions honestly. I'll need those answers to think."

"O-okay, you got it."

Lapis sighed, then unleashed her deluge of questions. Loren thought she might look quite diligent were she not half-naked. He waited in earnest for his own coat to dry.

Lapis's interrogation carried on until Loren's coat was dry as bones. By then, Lapis and Feuille's clothes were ready as well. Feuille slipped his shirt on as soon as he had the chance. As for Lapis, she didn't claim her clothes until she was satisfied with Cornet's interrogation. She got dressed with a conflicted look on her face.

"How was it?" Loren asked, having left the questioning up to her.

She shook her head a few times as if to jar her thoughts into order, and finally said, "First of all, this is that hidden fairy village we were looking for."

Loren had nursed a hunch from the moment Cornet mentioned the chieftain. It seemed his intuition was on point today. Despite their scramble for information, they had reached their destination before they found any leads.

This was good news, in a sense, but terrible news as well. There were no elves in sight, after all. The party had been searching for the hidden village of the fairies in the hopes of finding refugees from Feuille's settlement. They hadn't seen hide nor hair of any elf, and it wasn't as if the elves could be tucked away in the little fairy buildings.

Which meant the elves hadn't found sanctuary here.

"I checked, just to make sure," said Lapis. "None of the elves ever sought refuge here."

"Are there any other places like this?"

"Not as far as Ms. Cornet knew."

That didn't mean all hope was lost. Feuille might have expected his fellows to run to the fairy village, but that was hardly proof that they had. Perhaps some elves had fled to other settlements.

The party, unfortunately, didn't have the means to confirm this. At present, they only knew that there were no elves in the fairy village, save for Feuille.

"Everyone..."

Perhaps Feuille was the lone survivor. This came as a blow to the boy, but Loren and Lapis couldn't offer any words of comfort. They whispered to one another:

"He might've been incredibly lucky, being nabbed by those bandits."

"Mr. Loren, you shouldn't say that even if it's true."

In one corner was a mercenary—life and death were an every-day occurrence to Loren. A comrade might be right as rain one day and cold in the ground the next; he had experienced just that too many times.

In the other corner was a demon who couldn't have cared less about anything outside of her own interests.

Neither of them was completely oblivious, so they tried not to say anything careless enough to scar a soft child. To be honest, though, neither grasped the true depth of his shock, and neither could think of anything tactful to say.

"Umm, chin up," said Lapis. "The chieftain apparently sealed himself off behind a barrier in the back. If we want to kill him, we'll first have to break the barrier."

"Cornet and the other fairies can't break it?"

Fairies were supposed to possess a fair knack for magic. Couldn't they dispel a barrier or two on their own?

"Well, they would be able to do something about it if they made a serious effort," Lapis said.

"In that case..."

"But if they pour their magic into breaking the barrier, they wouldn't have the strength left to defeat the chieftain after."

Breaking the barrier to fight their chieftain would sap the fairies of all their mana. That had left Cornet at a standstill, even though she accepted the fact that the chieftain needed to go. She knew full well the extent of what the village's fairies could—or couldn't—accomplish. That was precisely why she needed the help of an outsider or two.

"Is Cornet actually someone important?" Loren asked.

"Important enough to rally the others."

Rally the others, hopefully, to follow her proposal. She wanted the village fairies to all work together to clear a path for Loren, so he could sally forth to slay a tiny chieftain.

"Hey, I hope I've got this wrong, but if everyone put together can only just barely break this one measly barrier, doesn't that mean this chieftain is about as strong as every other fairy here put together?"

"That would be the logical conclusion."

Fairies were already better than elves at magic. If it took an entire village of them to rival one chieftain, it wasn't hard to imagine how troublesome a foe he would be.

"Can we actually beat him?"

"I think it will work out if no one's watching," Lapis answered, all confidence.

Lapis hesitated to use her strength with an audience, and Scena similarly wouldn't wield her full power in front of others. Once they got rid of prying eyes, though, they could go at it without restraint. Both Lapis and Scena were incredibly powerful, and neither intended to fall short of some fairy chief.

"Well, even if someone decides to rubberneck, I think we can deceive them easily enough."

<I'll help out too! Secretly!>

Even holding back their true abilities, Loren thought a demon and a Lifeless King might still rival the chief. Both girls were fully capable of bringing nations to ruin.

Loren, meanwhile, could only swing around a sword. He was starting to see himself as little more than a second-string fighter, but both Lapis and Scena seemed to believe they could push him onto the front lines and summon miracles by cheering him on.

"So you're fine with taking Cornet's quest?" Loren asked.

"I am. We decided on a proper reward already."

He'd thought Lapis's interrogation session was merely to gather information, but it seemed she'd also bartered the details of a proper adventuring request.

She works fast, Loren thought.

"I tried making it sound like a big deal, but the reward won't be anything special. The fairies are like the elves; they use hardly any precious metals."

"They can't eat much either, not with bodies like that. I can't see them having enough to share with us."

"With that in mind, it's incredible that the chief managed to devour the supplies from the elf settlement," Lapis mused. "Does he have a stomach of iron, perhaps? Maybe incredibly potent gastric acid?"

"Who knows? So, what did you agree on?"

Fairies traded even less than elves did. Seeing as they didn't conduct any business with humans, it was hard to imagine the hidden village had anything of significant monetary value.

"Yes, about that. If we do manage to kill the chief, we'll be permitted to select one thing from the treasures the fairies have collected."

Lapis had made the deal hoping that some great valuable lay hidden among the shiny things the fairies regularly snatched up. Even if there wasn't anything really flashy, one gemstone would be enough to cover the costs of their expedition.

"Even if we don't find anything incredible, I'm hoping we can at least turn a profit with this job."

"Makes sense to me."

The fairies were in deep trouble, so Lapis could have leveraged their desperation to get the party more than one prize. Unfortunately, wrangling rewards through the exploitation of the weak left a sour taste in the mouth.

In the end, Lapis's proposal was a good compromise—Loren would be able to fight with a clear mind, and he wouldn't go into debt doing it.

"We're leaving Feuille here. Any objections?"

"None at all. That sounds obvious."

Feuille lifted his chin at this, but neither Loren nor Lapis had any intention of taking him to see the chief. It was entirely possible that Feuille would find himself thinking of the chieftain as the one who'd stolen his family from him. They couldn't say for sure, but it was a definite possibility. Perhaps Feuille wanted to get in at least one punch during the battle that would be his vengeance.

Despite this, they couldn't bring him. At the end of the day, the fairy chief could apparently birth his own brethren from elf corpses, and they had enough trouble to deal with already.

"Bear with me on this," Loren told the boy. "If we take you along, I'd have to protect you. If the chief made more fairies from you, we'd be attacked from both sides."

While Feuille looked dissatisfied, he silently hung his head. It seemed like Loren had gotten through to him.

With that decided, Cornet floated into their midst and asked about the request.

"I can't give any guarantees," Loren said.

Despite that, Cornet flew in happy circles around him. "We could never ask for that much. We're just happy to know you accepted."

He'd make himself dizzy if he followed her with his eyes, but he had to ask. "And we can count on you to do something about the barrier?"

"Of course you can! We'll help out to the best of our abilities!"

"And your request is to hunt down the chieftain, right? You want us to kill him."

It took some time before the answer fought free from behind her teeth. "That's what I'm asking."

It was impossible for Loren to know what went through Cornet's mind during that pause, nor how she resolved her own hesitation. Despite everything, she made her plea, and Loren nodded firmly.

7 A Battle to an Excavation

"**T**HE PLAN IS SIMPLE. This passage connects to where the chief is holed up. Ms. Cornet will lead the fairies to break the barrier. We'll follow the corridor, make contact with the chief, and fight him—and that should be the end of it."

"You make it sound so easy...not that there's anything else we can do, really."

Loren and Lapis stood before the passageway, ready to fulfill Cornet's request. Feuille had been left behind with the other fairies, as agreed.

"Now listen here. Don't let Feuille follow us no matter what." Loren needed to hammer this point home. "On the million-to-one chance he does come, we'll give up on killing the chief and run."

Cornet thumped her own chest, simply brimming with confidence. "Leave it to me. Worse comes to worst, I'll cast *Petrification* to stop him."

"You can be pretty vicious if you want to be, huh..."

This spell that Cornet so casually brought up was not the sort one typically used to detain a person. *Petrification* could turn living things to stone, and its victims were liable to spend an eternity as a statue unless it was dispelled. In short, it was a bona fide attack.

The fairies were better than the elves at magic, and Cornet seemed to be quite powerful among her people—if she cast a spell like that, Feuille would be done for before he went two steps.

"I'm sure I don't need to say this, but please don't kill him."

"Leave it to me!" Cornet agreed airily.

Loren didn't know how much he could trust a fairy taking that tone. A smidge of anxiety lingered.

"That aside, are you prepared, Mr. Loren?" Lapis asked.

Loren looked down to check himself over. He didn't need to prepare anything in particular. He always wore his clothes, boots, and leather armor. Aside from that, a black coat and the sword in his hands were all the equipment to his name.

The few other supplies he'd brought had been soaked during their unexpected swim. He doubted they'd be of any use in his fight with the chieftain, so he left them with Feuille.

"All clear on my end," he told Lapis.

"I see. Then Ms. Cornet, if you will."

"All right, here we go."

On Cornet's order, the magicians of the hidden village amassed their strength. Apparently. Loren could feel a pressure in the air, but there weren't any great beams of light, or explosions, or anything like that. How much magic they gathered, whatever that might mean, was well beyond him.

<That's just how magic is, Mister. It's pretty amazing to already feel pressure like this when it isn't an offensive spell.>

Loren was sure Scena's explanation was just fine, but he still didn't get it.

<Fine, there's no helping it,> she muttered, then opened her sense of sight to him.

Just a moment ago, Loren hadn't seen so much as a mystical sparkle, but now, it was as if the air itself warped around Cornet while she concentrated intently. The distortion rose so high that Loren had to look up to see the whole of it. Despite Cornet's small size, it was clear she was gathering something powerful.

<That's the mana she's amassing.>

"I understand now. This is pretty convenient."

<I have to completely synchronize my senses, so I can't pull it off for long. It chips away at your sanity,> Scena said, immediately severing the link. Loren's sight snapped back to normal.

"All right, here we go!"

Something fired from Cornet's body. Loren couldn't see it now, but from what he could tell, all the mana she had pulled in around her was released all at once. The shot rocketed down the corridor, and soon a sour stench began leaking out from farther in. Loren and Lapis instinctively turned their faces away, burying their noses in their raised sleeves.

"The barrier is broken!" Cornet wasn't flying so freely anymore. She teetered in the air, looking fatigued.

Mission accomplished, the path to the chieftain was revealed, but Loren sported quite the frown. "Why does it stink this bad?"

"I presume this putrid air is being emitted from their chieftain," Lapis said. "But...I really don't want to trace *this* back to its source."

Cornet panicked. "H-hey! That would dump me in a lot of hot water!"

"I'm only joking," Lapis said with a carefree laugh. "Now, Mr. Loren. Why don't you go ahead?"

"Hey, now. I know I'm the front-line fighter, but..."

Loren couldn't make a priest take point when they didn't know what awaited them, but that didn't mean he was going to forge bravely onward with a skip in his step. He also knew standing around would get him nowhere, so he girded his loins and took the first step—and Lapis followed just behind.

That glowing moss was sprouting from the walls off this corridor as well. There was no darkness to keep them paranoid, but that pungent odor grew stronger with each passing moment.

This smell is almost enough to break my will to fight, Loren thought, and that was when the passage opened up.

"Is this where the chief's supposed to be?"

Loren stepped warily into the new cave, his nose scrunched up in helpless protest at the wafting miasma. He'd assumed they'd recognize the source of the awful smell once they got close enough. But even though the chief had to be near, Loren hadn't the slightest idea what could be letting off such a stench.

It reminded him of the body odor of his mercenary comrades, especially after they had been ordered to attack day in and day out without any chance to clean themselves or their clothing, leading the aroma to concentrate and congeal ever further.

"Sweat, grime... There's a hint of something like rotten food mixed in." Lapis tried her best to identify the notes even as she covered her mouth and nose.

Perhaps there were other things mixed in there too, but determining that would mean further investigation, which they didn't have the time or the stomach for.

Lapis was the first to notice something meaningful. It was by the wall farthest from the entrance to the cave; at first, she couldn't tell what it was. After examining it for a long moment, she realized that perhaps it was what had become of a certain someone. She tugged on Loren's sleeve.

"Mr. Loren, is that... Just maybe..."

Loren followed her pointing finger, but the thing left him speechless.

What he saw was a skin-colored mountain. The wide cavern was also quite high, but the thing was so massive that Loren could imagine its top scraped the celling. What the hell could it be?

"Umm? No, it isn't... It can't be, right?"

The skin-colored mass was slick with some greasy substance. Wrinkles and folds sectioned off lumps of its greater mass, and its biggest section rose and fell steadily. This was, without a doubt, a breathing life-form.

As for what sort of creature it was, Loren had no answer. It was simply too foreign and grotesque, like a bulbous flesh plant had taken root in the gloom.

"Must be where the smell is coming from."

Its body glistened as if coated in oil, and the idea of touching it repulsed Loren. He reluctantly approached, prodding a distended bit with the tip of his boot. Lapis tried to stop him to no avail; he had drawn the giant organism's attention.

"Who... You who...?"

"It talks?!" Loren exclaimed.

It was undoubtedly a voice, but Loren had zero clue what part of the thing the voice had come out of. The blob had reacted to his poking, and though its words were disjointed, it spoke with purpose. Loren slowly backed off to whisper to Lapis, who was more than happy to get some distance from it.

"Lapis, what is that thing?"

"We came here to find the fairy chief, so I think you can answer your own question."

Loren wasn't completely clueless. But when he compared Cornet's report with this lump of flesh, well, he did the math and really didn't like the answer.

"You gotta be kidding me. This is the fairy chief?"

Sure, they'd been expecting to run into the chief down here, but all the fairies they'd met in the village had been palm-sized kids like Cornet. He couldn't imagine such dainty things taking on such a towering form.

"This is crazy! How in the hell is this supposed to be a fairy?!"

"Don't ask me," Lapis said.

Loren could only connect a few of the dots. "He gorged himself and fattened up..."

Neither of them had ever seen a fairy chieftain before, so they didn't know if he'd been a robust sort to begin with. He was a fairy, though, so they could assume a few things. Maybe he'd done this to himself eating all the food plundered from the elven settlements.

"But this is a bit much, don't you think?"

"He's passed the size where he can move on his own."

"Don't you think we could end this pretty easily, then?"

They had been told they'd be up against a fairy far stronger than any other in the hidden village. Loren had prepared himself for a demanding battle. Seeing as their opponent couldn't even move, the whole business was looking a lot easier.

In the next instant, that hope was snuffed out. Several red balls collided with the floor where Loren had stood just a moment before, sending out waves of spark and flame.

"It looks like he's not going down without a fight."

As it turned out, whether or not the fairy chieftain could move was totally irrelevant. The chief was a magician; as long as he was conscious, he could make full use of plenty of spells.

"It'll be the end of us if we don't take this seriously," Loren muttered, readying his sword.

The lump of flesh, either nervous for battle or gleeful to have found new food before it, jiggled its massive body. Its vile odor blossomed throughout the cave.

They had conceded the first blow to the fairy chieftain, but Loren's counterattack was vicious and swift. Lapis retreated a step to observe the situation as Loren rushed out with his sword aloft, slicing down at the mass.

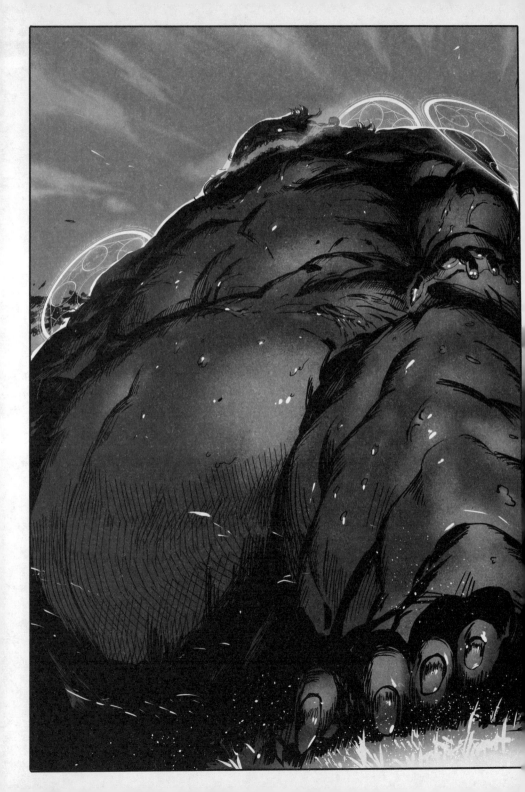

The flesh didn't look hard to cut, but Loren had learned plenty about the strength of magical protections. He made sure to put considerable strength into the first blow.

"Gree...?" The chieftain's response didn't even amount to a scream. Loren's slash cut deep, showering the area with blood.

"Looks like my attacks work. But..." He quickly dodged back.

The flesh around the cut swelled and slammed down where Loren had been standing. It made a sound like a wet rag slapped against the floor. The wound that Loren inflicted had widened on impact, covering the ground with even more flesh and blood, but the chief was undeterred.

"His senses are dulled, and he's so big," Loren said. "It doesn't seem like the attack did anything."

"Guh...yurt..."

It at least seemed aware that it had been wounded. It took every muscle in the chief's body for it to inch back from Loren. Loren was surprised to see it could move at all. He rushed in to follow up with another strike, but the chief paid him no heed and continued crawling along the floor.

"Is that supposed to be an attempt at running away?"

"I think so."

Lapis pointed at a nearby mountain of *stuff* that stood about as high as the chieftain. Loren had been so distracted by the monstrosity that he hadn't noticed anything else, but on closer inspection, it was a mound of animal carcasses from the Black Forest—elf corpses included—and it no doubt contributed to the horrid smell.

"I got a bad feeling about this."

"It's not even a feeling. It's a reality."

Lapis's expression was scrunched up into something unpleasant. The chief paid his visitors no heed, crawling up to the mountain and shoving its face into it. It clung to the sides as if for dear life, filling the air with godawful noises as it chewed through all manner of substances hard and soft.

"It's eating...right?"

"There's no doubt about it."

When injured, it sought out food for recovery. That was understandable, in a way, but not the sort of thing to do when your enemies were still standing around. Loren, looking at his foe, felt rather fed up himself.

"I understand why you're making that face," said Lapis. "But look, the cuts are closing up."

She was right—the wounds Loren had inflicted sealed themselves closed at unimaginable rates. New flesh spanned the gashes left by his sword, bulging out and around until the chief was left whole and even larger than before.

"Is this thing immortal as long as it keeps eating?" Loren asked.

"I'm not so sure. In any case, it doesn't have an endless supply of food."

Wrestling with the detestable notion that he would have to keep chipping away until it ran out of snacks, Loren unleashed another attack on the chief's body. His blade cleaved through flesh, forming a gouge that sealed itself up before Loren's eyes as the chief continued to binge. The second round of healing made the chief bigger yet.

Maybe cutting isn't enough, Loren thought. After his next slice, he turned his blade sideways and carved down. This both widened the wound and lopped off a portion of the giant's body, sending a massive hunk of meat flying through the air. *That should hurt him more than a slash.*

The moment the severed flesh hit the ground, it split into several smaller segments. Each formed into palm-sized fairies, and each fairy launched itself at Loren to attack. Loren hadn't expected enemies to birth themselves from a blob of fat, and he failed to counter them in time. He was forced to take his left hand off his blade to try to protect his neck.

Several newly born fairies bit into his arm all at once.

<*Energy drain!*> Scena cried the moment before their small teeth could pierce his skin.

She stole enough life energy to instantaneously halt their vital processes. They fell to the ground like flies, and Loren immediately backed off, offering Scena his thanks.

"This is more trouble than it's worth. Cut something off and it becomes a fairy."

"Let it swirl before mine eyes, o crimson flames, ye storm and burst. *Firestorm!*"

As Loren cursed, Lapis unleashed the magic she had been preparing behind him. A whirlwind of flames burst from the ground, coiling around the chief's body, and Loren was forced to hold up his hand to shield his face from the heat.

Beyond his hand was the thoroughly scorched chief, and yet Lapis frowned somberly even before the spell ended.

"Too much moisture. He's not burning."

Sure enough, the giant still stood even after the flames receded. His skin was crisped, and parts of him were charcoaled and crumbling, but new flesh simply welled up from beneath. His blackened bits sloughed off to reveal new skin, glossy and damp.

"What do we do about this? Do I just keep carving him up?"

"Can you do anything with Ms. Scena's energy drain?" Lapis suggested.

As energy drain sucked away life force without inflicting any wounds, perhaps it would work against such a massive monster as well.

Despite the skill's theoretical potential, Scena insisted that she couldn't—rather, that she wouldn't.

<*Please cut me some slack! I'll use it to defend you from the smaller fairies, but... Sorry, Mister. I really don't want to use it on the main body,*> she pleaded feebly.

The chief rained down more flaming bullets as he ate. Loren took a few with the flat of his blade while pushing Scena to explain the problem.

<*I figured it out when I sucked the fairies dry... The chief's life force isn't the best. To be blunt, he tastes disgusting.*>

Lapis couldn't hear Scena, so Loren was on his own; he had no idea how to make his case. This was the first time she'd said anything about life energy having a flavor—and what did she mean by disgusting? A living man like him couldn't possibly imagine it.

<*It's a first for me too, so I don't know how to word it... Umm, do you want me to try explaining?*>

"Forget it."

What point was there in making her thoroughly detail how terrible it was? There was nothing to be gained. Still, Loren was shocked that the fairy chieftain possessed life force so off-putting that even a Lifeless King didn't want it.

"What's the word, Mr. Loren?"

"This guy apparently tastes awful."

"Oh... Then tell her not to force herself."

Lapis gave up on the idea so easily that Loren had to wonder why.

"You're just accepting that explanation?"

"Why wouldn't I?"

Meanwhile, the chief continued his meal, but also continued shooting rounds of fireballs at the new pests. Lapis drew a quick seal in front of her chest and softly chanted, "O god of knowledge, safeguard us from those that mean us harm. *Protection from Magic.*"

A faintly glowing semi-transparent membrane bubbled up around them. When the chieftain's fireballs hit the barrier, they fizzled out like sparks hitting a bucket of water.

The hulking mass shook irritably as the chief realized his attacks were pointless, but Lapis chanted on. "May god's invisible hand smite down our foes. *Force.*"

Her chant summoned a fragment of a miracle. A massive ball of power, proportional to her devotion, struck the chief's body. It was as if a god had truly lowered a fist from on high; the impact formed a crater and sent blood splashes to every corner. Yet Lapis, who had unleashed such an attack, seemed dissatisfied.

"I failed to crush him. I lack discipline, it seems."

"Is it that sort of blessing?"

It would be impossible to crush this giant without considerable force; the spell's incantation seemed a little too short for it to be that useful.

"Oh, not at all. The blessing normally deals about as much damage as a macho man punching with all his might."

"Why would you expect it to crush this thing, then?"

"I mean, you know, I'm such a pious and faithful young priest, after all."

Look who's talking, thought Loren as he dealt more blows. Each strike cut deftly into the chief's body, yet the flesh immediately regenerated. He couldn't shake off the feeling that this was a fruitless endeavor.

"You won't find many priests out there as strongly devoted as I. Honest."

"You make a good point."

The god of knowledge was a bit different from his divine peers. As long as Loren kept that in mind, he could see Lapis being a priest who was a cut above the rest.

"All right then. Slicing doesn't work, smacking doesn't work. What now?"

"Well, I'd really like to try burning it again, but..." Lapis trailed off, glancing around.

Loren cut through another part of the chief's body that had been coming down to crush them. He didn't know why she was holding back.

"If we were outside, I wouldn't hesitate to use my full firepower."

"Oh. Yeah... This ain't the place for that."

They weren't completely sealed off from the world, but the cave's ventilation wasn't the best. If Lapis mustered enough strength to burn something that large, the heat and stagnant air would do terrible things to them.

"But then what... Ah?"

Loren stopped himself. Lapis followed his gaze, wondering what had happened, and saw that the food—though one hesitated to call it that—had nearly run dry. It was impressive that the chieftain had eaten such a staggering amount while fighting them, but now that the hoard was gone, there was only one place for him to turn his appetite.

"You think we're next on the menu?"

"If only it weren't so."

Up to that point, the chief had barely seemed to have a grasp on his surroundings or the fight. He was wounded, he healed himself, and healing made him hungry, but he hadn't appeared to think of anything beyond that cycle. Now that the food was gone, there was nothing left to shove into his gaping maw.

His attacks would grow fiercer. That wasn't a welcome development when they still didn't have a plan.

"Seriously, what do we do?"

There was no telling where the chief's eyes were in that mass of flesh, but they could feel his attention gradually shift toward them. Lapis sounded truly troubled as she looked up at the encroaching creature.

"This is no time to just stare at the thing!"

Loren grabbed Lapis and jumped. Some protrusion of the chief's body crashed down where she had been, hitting so hard, the protrusion burst into blood. Loren swung, cutting off another large chunk. The chunk fell, bursting into countless fairies that darted after them.

<*Energy drain... Erk... This is terrible...*> Scena complained, but her powers did promptly get rid of the fairy problem.

However, the chieftain wormed his way over to the fallen fairies, absorbing them into his mass.

"He's finally started eating himself."

"This is getting more pointless by the second," Lapis murmured from under Loren's arm. She sounded as if it had nothing to do with her, and Loren hardly had time to answer her.

He was busy using his left hand, again and again, slicing through the arms of flesh coming at him. If he managed to sever those pieces, they instantly turned into fairies that fired at him like bullets. There was no end in sight.

<*I know I can't actually vomit in this state, but I feel like I'm going to...*>

With no physical form, Scena had no means to relieve her nausea. If she did manage to throw up, astrally speaking, she might, at most, vent off some of the chieftain's life force, but the disgusting feeling would remain.

"We won't get anywhere without a plan!"

Cut and cut as Loren may, it was as if the giant had no sense of pain. The chieftain was rather impressive for attacking at such a rapid rate, though Loren was nothing to scoff at either, using only his left hand to swing his heavy weapon and block every attempt.

The sound of flesh against steel rang out without pause, bits of fat and blood flying. The aftermath dashed red stains onto Lapis's white robes.

"I'll have to buy new ones when we get back..."

"Is this really the time to talk about that?!"

"Vestments are pretty expensive, you know. They use high-quality cloth."

"Worry about your life more than your clothes!"

Loren wanted to gain more distance before he let go of Lapis and used both hands, but the chieftain's attacks gave him no chance. The moment they began trading blows, he could no longer stop. He considered just dropping her, but if he abandoned Lapis in the midst of the chief's endless assault, she'd become a target. Her slender body didn't look up to handling the sheer mass of it.

She was a demon, of course, and it was just as likely that she could fend off the attacks with a pinky finger. Loren couldn't say for sure, and he couldn't bring himself to take the bet. Her life was too much to gamble with.

"Lay off a bit, would you?!" he shouted.

A strange sensation was beginning to elbow its way into his mind. When this feeling overcame him, Loren could push himself to perform much greater feats of offensive prowess than usual, but it would also place a time limit on the fight. That would all be well and good if he could defeat the chieftain before he collapsed;

if he couldn't, he would be left unable to move or, really, to do anything about being devoured.

"Mr. Loren, why don't you follow my instructions for a bit?" Lapis proposed, looking up from under his arm. He barely glanced at her, keeping his eyes on the fight. She twisted her body, straining herself into quite a difficult posture to place a hand on his chest.

"I'm going to do something a little reckless. If you can learn this technique, your combat abilities will grow by leaps and bounds."

"What are you getting at?! You're not modifying me, are you?"

"I'm not. I couldn't without the proper tools and facilities, anyway. What do you think I am?" she grumbled, her hand fumbling around his torso. It felt a bit ticklish at first, though soon he began to feel the warmth from her palm.

It was a warmth beyond body heat, piercing through his skin and muscles into the hollows of his body. It felt as if she were pulling something out from deep within him, and though he never stopped defending himself from the chieftain's attacks, he shuddered.

"What's this...?"

"From what I've seen, that last-resort rampage of yours converts your life force and stamina into energy. However, the conversion process rapidly depletes your strength, and it's actually quite dangerous for you."

The hilt of his sword let out a harsh grating noise: the sound of Loren gripping it stronger than he ever had before. The next attack he unleashed at the chieftain was faster, more powerful.

As if to back up Lapis's hypothesis, this slash tore far deeper into the barriers of flesh, and the chief winced in pain for the first time. The mass retreated ever so slightly, allowing Loren some breathing room.

"Wh-whoa."

"This is the sort of self-reinforcement any demon could pull off. It's not quite as good as a blessing, since you can only do it to yourself, but memorize this feeling."

In the time his attack bought them, Lapis slipped out of his hold and jumped behind him. She knew Loren would have a hard time exhibiting his full might while carting her around—it was time to leave this to him.

"Once you remember how the mana feels as it courses through your body, you should be able to call it up again on your own. I forced the process out of you this time, but don't forget the sensation."

Taking care to heed her explanation and the feeling she'd drawn through him, Loren took a sharp step toward the chief and loosed an upward swing with both hands on his sword. Whether he had too much momentum or had merely misjudged the distance, the sword's tip dug into the ground and raised sparks as the blade was practically sucked into the chief's body, leaving a long, deep slice.

"Yurt! I yurt!"

"Shut it! I'll carve you up, so quit running!"

Striking upward took too much time and energy, so this time, Loren sliced from top to bottom. Two parallel slashes lopped off another large chunk of flesh. As before, it transformed into fairies. They all rushed at Loren to bite him, but Loren used the flat of his blade to intercept them.

The sword became a two-ton flyswatter. One swing flattened their small bodies.

With another step forward, Loren stabbed deep into the chief and mercilessly twisted the blade. The chieftain winced back, his screech rising in volume and pitch. Loren stayed there a while before pulling out his blade. He nearly dropped the sword entirely when he noticed a human hand grasped around the midpoint of the sword.

"What the hell?!"

Given the size, the hand couldn't have belonged to a fairy. It was about as large as Lapis's. Loren shuddered a bit, but continued pulling the blade back. For some reason, the blade's edge didn't break the hand's skin. It followed the sword smoothly as he pulled his weapon from the gaping hole he'd carved.

"This is grossing me out..."

"Mr. Loren, what are you pulling out of the chieftain's body?"

A lone right arm stretched out of the chieftain, who, eerily enough, had stopped attacking. The arm's skin was smooth and not terribly muscular. Just going off the shape, Loren presumed it belonged to a woman, but to see it sprouting from within that giant thing was off-putting no matter how he sliced it.

"What do I do about this?"

"Do you...really have any option besides pulling on it?"

Loren peeked up at the chieftain. It was as if all those previous attacks had been a dream—the massive lump of flesh was frozen, not even twitching. He remained a tad disturbed by the woman's hand extending from the wound, but seeing no other course of action, he buried his sword into the chief's flesh and hesitantly grabbed the arm with both hands. Then he braced his knees and pulled.

The chief's body didn't put up much resistance, and the owner of the arm obviously wanted to escape. It wasn't long before the muscles and fat had been torn through. The hand gave way to a shoulder, then a head.

This head, covered in blood and grease, sported blonde hair, nearly white. As they burst into a violent coughing fit, spitting up blood and who knew what else, Loren hurriedly let go, retrieved his sword, and retreated to Lapis.

The person he had pulled out of the fairy chieftain continued vomiting and emitting sounds that weren't the least bit elegant. Once she had spit everything up, panting heavily, she wiped off her mouth with her free hand and suddenly pulled herself out up to the waist.

Her body was obviously, or perhaps expectedly, naked, and she possessed all the features of a young woman.

She made no effort to hide her shapely curves as she wiped the viscera off her face and sniffed her hands. Eventually, she braced her palms against the fairy chieftain's flesh and hauled herself the rest of the way out.

"Wowee, this is just terrible. I reek, I'm slimy, I'm all covered in blood. What a waste of my good looks, eh?"

The woman twisted about to look herself over. Soon, her eyes turned to Loren and Lapis.

"Thanks a bunch, sir and madam," she called out to them with a jovial smile. "I can't tell you how worried I was when I was released from my seal only to end up in there. Seems these folks here hardly cook their food at all—they eat it raw, I'm telling you. And they eat rotten things, kitchen waste! I thought I was gonna die, eating all that garbage."

She laughed, but Loren readied his sword the moment he saw her eyes. She looked human enough, but those irises were a vivid purple.

"Oh, don't be like that. I'm not plannin' on doin' nothin' here. Not when I'm feelin' all grateful. If you didn't haul me out, I'd have had to stay with the big guy for all eternity."

Loren couldn't bring himself to speak.

"Might I ask your name?" Lapis asked.

The woman looked at Lapis curiously before folding her arms in front of her chest. "We got an odd one here, but whatever. I'm Gula Gluttonia. They used to call me the dark god of gluttony or somethin', and some adventurer sealed me away because of it. Now here I am, revived. That a good enough answer for you?"

Lapis nodded and piled on another question. "You don't have any intention of quietly letting yourself be resealed, do you?"

"Not really. I wanna wash my mouth out after eatin' so much filth, and I've been sealed for such a long time, you know? Can't I stretch out a bit?"

Lapis stared at the woman called Gula for a bit, but eventually cast down her eyes and replied, "As you wish."

"That so? Then I'll be takin' my leave. Oh, right, right. What's yer name, mister?"

The conversation was suddenly jerked in Loren's direction. He was taken aback, but he answered sincerely, "It's Loren."

"Loren... So you're Loren, eh? Then Loren, I really am grateful for what you did today. I'll repay you one of these days. Well, see ya."

Before he could say anything else, Gula smiled, waved, and sank into the solid ground as if it were a pool of water. She was gone without a trace.

All that remained was the body of the fairy chieftain, crumbling and rotting as if it had been left there for days. Its liquefied, rancid meat began to ooze along the ground.

"Why's it doing that?" Loren asked.

"Who knows? He was almost fully assimilated with that dark god. Now that the connection to her has been severed, it seems the chieftain went and died on us."

And it was just as she said: the fairy chieftain was a lump of rotting meat. The scent the carcass emitted made Loren want to run, not investigate further. If they stuck around, they'd experience sights and smells that would scar them for life, so the pair hastily retreated back down the passage from which they had come.

EPILOGUE
Returning to Nothing

ULTIMATELY, the chieftain's death was confirmed several days after Loren and Lapis returned to the fairy village. Based on their firsthand account, the fairies held hope that the chief was well and truly done for, but Cornet wanted to be sure. Understandable, but it left Lapis and Loren stuck in the forest, waiting around until they could receive their rewards.

"We're saving on room and board, I guess."

Loren lived most of his life crossing from battlefield to battlefield, so it didn't bother him if he couldn't return to town. Lapis grumbled a bit, but Cornet had insisted and Loren accepted, so she relented and bottled up her complaining.

That being said, the fairy-kind village was made for people of a completely different stature. There was nowhere to house two grown humanoids, and they were forced to camp out a few days and nights in their tents and sleeping bags.

"We're camping out, and the food's... You know..."

Evil god of gluttony or not, Gula had been spot on; fairies

rarely ever cooked their food. Lapis and Loren were mostly given raw fruits and wild plants. This was a bit much for the pair, so they had no choice but to build a fire on the edge of the settlement, subsisting off their rations and fish skewered in the lake.

It took so long to confirm the chieftain's death because of the condition of his body. As soon as the gluttonous god had left it, it started rotting at a rapid pace, and it was soon so decomposed that it was impossible to determine whether the corpse belonged to the chief or some other creature entirely. It wasn't as if the fairies were impervious to the smell either.

With little choice in the matter, the fairies gathered up flowers and fragrant herbs to keep themselves sane. They incinerated the rotten mean bit by bit, collecting anything that could serve as evidence until, finally, they reached the conclusion that the massive thing was undoubtedly their chief.

"You really saved us there," Cornet said. "I don't know how to repay you."

She'd apparently made such a good show at rallying the fairies that she'd been appointed their next chieftain. Not that any of them particularly cared who their leader was.

As for the elves, they hadn't yet been completely annihilated. Cornet managed to establish contact with another elf settlement in the Black Forest, and Feuille would be entrusted to them. He'd lost his family along with everyone he knew, but as an elf, he still had a long life ahead of him. Loren could only pray that time would eventually heal the wounds on his heart.

"Now about your reward."

Cornet led them to a sort of warehouse in the corner. With a heave and a ho, the other fairies were hard at work ferrying out its contents. This was the only way to examine the stockpile, as neither Lapis nor Loren could enter the building, but it took the fairies a good deal of sweat and tears to haul out all the treasures contained within.

"As promised, please pick any one thing and take it with you."

Lapis immediately began scouring the hoard. Loren, for his part, did nothing, simply watching over her as she picked up various articles and carefully appraised them. It wasn't like he had the skill set to tell which gemstones were more expensive than others. Leaving it to the ever-knowledgeable Lapis was therefore the most efficient way to make the most out of their reward. But after she had scanned through quite a bit of the haul, he saw that her hands had stopped.

"What's wrong?" he asked her. She turned to him like a rusty hinge. Wondering what could have possibly made her so stiff, he peeked over her shoulder and grimaced. "That's..."

Lapis was clenching a translucent purple gem that didn't look particularly valuable. It was decently large but had been arbitrarily faceted, and it didn't look like the sort of thing Lapis would be shocked by. However, Loren dimly recognized it. He cocked his head, trying to remember.

"Mr. Loren, this..." She sounded lost, and Loren abruptly recalled what it was, his eyes widening in surprise.

"Is it really...that?"

He thought back to their last request at the adventurer training academy. The thing Lapis had nonchalantly obtained on the lowest floor and brought home with her had been identical to what she held in her hands.

"What part is it?"

"My right hand, probably..."

This gem was what had become of one of the limbs Lapis's parents had snatched away from her before hiding them around the world. Lapis had regained her left arm at the academy, and it seemed her right arm had been in the fairy storehouse.

"I believe they found it somewhere in the Black Forest and picked it up..."

"That's convenient."

Lucky. She found what she was looking for, thought Loren, but Lapis was looking more troubled than ever.

"What's wrong? Say you want it."

He didn't know what other treasures there were to find, but Lapis's body parts couldn't be bought for money. He didn't see any other option and thought she would jump at the opportunity. However, Lapis's opinion seemed to differ.

"I'll give up on it this time."

"Why's that?"

"We can't make any money off of this. Therefore, there is nothing to split, and you gain nothing, Mr. Loren," Lapis said. She made to return the gem to the mountain of treasures, but Loren snatched it away from her. Before she could do anything, he held it up to Cornet.

"Cornet, we'll take this as our reward."

"You got it."

"Hey! Mr. Loren!" Lapis protested.

Loren put the newly obtained gemstone in her hand. "If you're that worried about it, why don't you split the reward by knocking a bit off my debt?"

"But...if I do that..."

His debt would go down, sure, but they still wouldn't make any money off the expedition. Loren might make up a bit of his deficit, and Lapis would regain some of her body, but money-wise they'd remain at zero.

"We've got the reward from the monster hunt they tallied up in town. That should be enough profit for us."

"About that..." She looked at him apologetically, and Loren tilted his head.

Did something happen to it? he wondered. He was right on the money.

"The certificate was in my bags."

"What about them?"

"Remember how we jumped in the water before we reached the village?"

Loren finally caught on. They had been underwater so long that their clothes and bags had been soaked to the core, and it was easy to guess what had happened to the paper.

"It got wet..."

"Yes, sopping wet. I tried drying it, but the ink had blurred, and it is essentially unreadable."

"That's, well... Tough luck."

But there hadn't been any other option at the time, as far as Loren was concerned. The results were unfortunate, but he couldn't blame anyone. He gave up on the matter.

"Hey, I've got less debt, you've got your body. Let's just say it ended well, eh? Even if you gave up this time, you'd have to come back for it eventually, right? Saves you the trouble."

Loren placed a hand on her head, bringing an end to the debate. Lapis still looked lost, but she soon gave him a smile, holding the gemstone to her chest.

"I'll cast magic on you properly, so you don't get wet on the way out," Cornet assured them.

"Please do. Wait, is the waterway the only exit?"

"The other one is blocked by the chief's body."

That was yet another thing Loren could do little about, and he gave up worrying about it as well. It was either diving into water or doing something about the decaying flesh. The water was far less painful, and with Cornet's magic, it was hardly worth any thought at all.

"Then we'll be heading out."

"Loren, Lapis, I'm really grateful. If you two hadn't done something about the chief, we also might have been taken by that strange power and attacked someone," Cornet said as she circled around the two of them, casting her spells. "I won't forget this debt."

"We took a quest, you paid the reward. We're even."

"Even so. You had the option to pretend you hadn't seen a

thing and put the forest behind you. I, Cornet of fairy-kind, am truly grateful. Don't forget that."

"Sure, got it. If we ever meet again."

Cornet saw them off with a sad wave before Loren and Lapis jumped back down into the waterway. On their way to the village, Loren had vividly felt the water's cold against his skin. Now with the magic Cornet cast on him, he no longer felt an unpleasant dampness in his clothes, nor the cool sensation of water whatsoever.

"If only it was like this every time..."

He hadn't taken a guild quest this time around, so he hadn't failed. The certificate had been rendered illegible, so he didn't have high hopes for that, but his only losses had been the equipment and food supplies needed to get them to the forest. That hadn't been so pricey, really.

In fact, they had both gained something, Lapis a piece of herself, and Loren a reduction on his debt. What's more, he usually found himself in a hospital bed at the end of every quest, but this time he was still conscious, and he didn't feel much pain at all.

"I feel like we're missing something..." Lapis murmured.

"Nope."

"Curses, next time for sure."

"Who the hell are you supposed to be?!"

"You say that, but the truth is, you actually like the hospital bed."

"I don't, just get swimming already!"

They could talk underwater thanks to Cornet's magic, and tease each other as well. Loren gave Lapis a light push to get her moving. Still, he wasn't badly injured, he was still awake, and he hadn't faced a financial loss.

Not bad, once in a while, he thought as he slowly swam after her.

LAPIS HERE. The other day, I coincidently ran into a friend in town and told them, "I'm a perfectly normal demon, aren't I?" Then guess what they did. They looked at me with pity and snorted.

It was mildly irritating, but that look must have come from their failing eyesight. Yes, of course. I sent them some incredibly effective eye drops, along with a letter that placed a serious curse on whoever opened it. We're all demons here, so no one's going to die. Probably.

There's a surprising number of us mixed into human society, going completely unnoticed. We're so good-looking and friendly, so why are we so hated? I posed this question to the open air, and Mr. Loren, who just so happened to be passing by, answered, "It's probably your personality."

That was a bit discouraging.

Incidentally, about my partner, Mr. Loren. His success rate as an adventurer seems to be on a downward spiral, so I was thinking

I needed to do something for him. It's not like there weren't any adequate quests, but rather than having him complete one of those, I thought I ought to teach him the joys of being an adventurer. This was, without a doubt, out of the kindness of my heart.

The idea that came to me was to put him to work without taking a formal job. That way, there would be no risk of failure—indeed, success was the only option. What's more, since it wasn't a quest, there wouldn't be any interlopers mixed in, and we'd be all alone together.

That's certainly what you call killing two birds with one stone.

At least, that's what I thought, but someone attacked the rest town we were supposed to stop at. Is that bad luck? Were we born under the wrong star? It was a small town, but everything had been taken and everyone had been slaughtered—that must have required quite a few people to accomplish.

According to Mr. Loren, it would have taken at least two hundred, and he guessed that they were mercenaries who had turned bandit. That made them incredibly dangerous.

I thought we should get rid of them wholesale before they caused any more trouble, and while I was anxious about our own manpower, Mr. Loren came forth with a certain confession. The daughter of a city chancellor we'd failed to save on another quest, who had been turned into an undead by a certain someone, had borrowed some space in Mr. Loren's astral body, and she could still make use of her powers.

We had practically won at that point. It didn't matter how many hundreds of bandits there were. If we could use the powers of the Lifeless King without a care about who was watching, then as long as we could cut down the first few, the rest could be left to the low- to mid-ranking undead.

The scary thing about the undead is how death begets death, and those new deaths will bring about more like a contagion. May those bandits feel the weight of stealing our beds and dinner in hell.

Incidentally, the undead could also be counted on to kill every living thing they came across—which meant no witnesses. After that, we just had to feign ignorance on the matter. The only downside to the undead is that we can't always rely on them. What a problem.

We managed to devastate the bandits, but our joyous looting led us to a bit of trouble—an elf child. I had Mr. Loren check properly, and it was a boy.

(You can't expect me to check the sex of someone I've just met. I'm a maiden, after all.)

His name was Feuille, apparently, and a few misunderstandings led to me stepping on him. From what I heard during Loren's patient questioning session, he was a victim of one of those hackneyed kidnapping plots.

Feuille hailed from the same Black Forest we were headed to anyway, so it only made sense to return him there. Still, I was well aware that elves are hardheaded, despite being so frail. I hoped he didn't misunderstand and attack us. Oh, I need to keep this a secret from Nym.

Something good happened at the inn, by the way. When we led Mr. Feuille around, the owner mistook us for a family. He seemed to be quite the discerning man, so I secretly prayed for his business to flourish. I'm sure that the god of knowledge has some good finance tips in his needlessly expansive pool of information.

Of course, Mr. Loren immediately denied the family thing. He sure is stubborn, good grief.

We took Mr. Feuille back to his settlement, but there was something clearly off about the Black Forest. Strangest of all was a pack of Forest Wolves we came across. They don't usually form packs so big, and they aren't usually so tenacious.

Perhaps Mr. Feuille and I looked especially delicious, but those wolves didn't back down when burned or cut, and they had a strange air about them.

The oddities didn't end there. While we walked through the forest the next day, we were met with scene upon scene that made me question if we had wandered into hell. They were sights that made me believe the elves residing in such a place had to be absolute degenerates to enjoy living there, but according to Mr. Feuille, that was not how the forest as he remembered it being.

I'm actually a little impressed. It seems trouble follows Mr. Loren wherever he goes.

The most valuable player here had to be Ms. Scena—the Lifeless King. That energy drain ability she deployed was able to kill any bugs and small animals almost instantly, and she could even suck the bigger animals dry without much difficulty.

The perfect bug repellent. Truly, what a profit we could turn if we could arrange for one Lifeless King in every household. As expected of the highest form of undead.

We proceeded with Ms. Scena's assistance, but once we arrived at Mr. Feuille's settlement, there was something odd there as well. The settlement was an empty shell, and the lone survivor was being attacked by fairies for some reason.

They attacked us too, and we still had no idea what was happening. Ms. Scena's power proved useful yet again. They really are amazing, those Lifeless Kings. They're usually walking calamities, but you really couldn't find yourself a more reliable ally.

Nevertheless, the only mental image I had of fairies was of them fluttering around flowery meadows like they do in fairy tales. The bloodstained variety will probably come up in my nightmares. I pray I don't see such horrid dreams, but if I do, I'll have Mr. Loren comfort me.

Mr. Feuille's settlement seemed utterly devastated, but according to him, they had an emergency evacuation point. We encountered another fairy attack as we were searching for a way to find it.

It was quite the horrific spectacle to see fairies burst out of elf corpses, but it was even more terrifying to be chased down by them. Though I could have, I didn't burn them down with the forest. I'm certainly a demon, which makes me better at magic than humans, but I gravitate toward fire and lightning spells, and I haven't really learned any plain ones.

As for how you run away from countless fairies, common sense would dictate jumping into the water. It's a simple method that works on bees as well. Of course, it only works when there's a deep enough body of water nearby, and as luck would have it for us, there was: a beautiful lake with lovely clear water.

I've heard that fish can't live in water when it's too clean, which meant there was little risk of us being attacked underwater. We all happily took the dive.

Incidentally, I am a capable demon, so I properly deployed a spell to breathe underwater, but Mr. Loren didn't notice at first. He was probably desperately holding his breath until Ms. Scena told him. How cute.

In the water, we met a fairy who had maintained her sanity. Her name was Ms. Cornet. As we listened to her story, I had to strip off my wet clothing, and Mr. Loren saw this and that, but it didn't really bother me. In fact, I thought he would get more of an eyeful, but he turned bright red and looked away and said he wasn't fond of shameless women, so I couldn't even tease him about it.

According to Ms. Cornet, the chieftain of the fairies went crazy after picking up a certain item, then went around killing and eating elves. We asked what that item was, and the description bore a close resemblance to something we had seen before.

That item was the most likely cause of the madness.

I wanted to cure him if I could, but unfortunately, I couldn't think of any effective means to so, and the chieftain couldn't be left to his own devices. We had no choice but to kill him.

We left Mr. Feuille with Ms. Cornet and used Ms. Cornet's help to reach the chieftain, but by then, the chieftain wasn't even recognizable as a fairy.

How should I put this? He looked like no more than a lump of flesh. Perhaps because Mr. Loren recognized that killing the chieftain would be for his own good, he got right to attacking. But the chieftain could still use magic, as it turned out, and fairies were born from any parts cut off of him. He was a troublesome foe.

What's more, according to Loren, the chief's life force tasted too terrible for Scena to use her energy drain.

I tried using a priestly blessing, but before the chieftain's giant mass, even the powers of a devout believer were far from enough to deal a decisive blow. This was no laughing matter.

We cycled through our options until finally, the chieftain recognized us as food. As a means of recovering from what seemed like a standstill, I initiated Mr. Loren into the traditional demon art of self-reinforcement.

This way, he would be able to raise his combat abilities without having to collapse every time he did so, and all that remained was to carve the chief to pieces.

It was at that point that something strange emerged from a hole Mr. Loren had cut open: a woman's arm.

None of us knew what was going on as Mr. Loren took the hand and pulled out a naked woman. She was, drumroll please, the dark god with authority over gluttony, a Ms. Gula Gluttonia. Don't get me wrong, I knew from the moment Ms. Cornet mentioned the item that drove the chieftain mad that a dark god was probably involved. I just hadn't expected her to be *fused* with him.

The dark god said all sorts of things with a strange accent and ran away before I fully understood the situation. With their link severed, the chief was unfortunately left behind to die.

How should I say this? What an incredible bother.

Still, with all that went on, we managed to do what Ms. Cornet asked of us, and as a reward, I received a clear gemstone the fairies had coincidentally happened to pick up—one that was a part of myself, so to speak.

The precise reward was to pick one thing out of their storehouse, and taking this thing would mean that Mr. Loren would receive no reward, so I thought to give up on it. But he insisted.

The proof of our monster hunt had been completely ruined when we jumped in the water, so we had absolutely no alternative source of income, but he said he didn't care.

This is troublesome. He's raising my affection points again.

But he really is a good person, Mr. Loren. Truly.

Now then, I think I'm going to end things here for now. I'll only note that this time, even after he fought quite a bit, Mr. Loren didn't end up in the hospital.

This is supposed to be a good thing, but for some reason, there's this feeling in my chest. I feel as if we're lacking something—I don't exactly know how to describe it. No, it's not like I want him to get injured, but it's kinda sorta becoming a habit of mine to watch him lay in bed after a job well done.

I should really do something about that.

For now, I'll put aside this feeling that I cannot describe and lower my pen until our next adventure.

THE Strange Adventure OF A Broke MERCENARY

Afterword

To all newcomers, it's a pleasure to meet you. To you old-timers, long time no see. My name is Mine, and this makes it four times that I've greeted the audience for this series. How is everyone doing?

There is a deep, dark ditch to cross between the third and fourth volume of a series. It's always a Herculean task to span it, and I'm grateful that this work managed to publish its fourth volume.

This is entirely thanks to all the readers who picked up this book, and you all have my deep, heartfelt gratitude. I pray for your continued patronage.

Last afterword, I secretly asked the readers for ideas to put into the afterwords, but at the present moment, I have not received a single submission. I'm sure you all think little old Mine is better off just writing whatever he wants at the end. Yes, I'm sure I'll be very happy once I convince myself of that. Salvation comes to those who believe. Or was that salivation? English is hard.

We're nearing the end now.

To everyone in Hobby Japan's editing department; to the proofreaders, the marketing team, and the designers; to peroshi-sama who keeps providing wonderful illustrations; and to my editor K-sama who always spares time for my phone calls: truly, thank you.

And my deepest thanks to you readers. I pray that your patronage may bring us together again.

—Mine